SUMMER BABY

BETH LABONTE

Copyright © 2017 Beth Labonte

All rights reserved. Except as permitted under U.S. Copyright Act of 1976, no part of this publication may be reproduced, distributed, or transmitted in any form or by any means, or stored in a database or retrieval system, without the prior written permission of the publisher.

First Edition (June 2017)

www.bethlabonte.com

❀ Created with Vellum

*For the real Richard & Joan.
Forgive me.*

TRYING

1

Why a *smiley* face?

Whichever sadistic, pea-brained scientist invented this thing—this ovulation predictor kit—they knew quite well that it wasn't going to be used by anybody in the mood to have a smug little smiley face peering up at them from the bathroom sink. They should have used the eye-rolling emoji; the kind that says, *You honestly expect me to have sex with my husband again?* Or perhaps the one with the little black X's over the eyes, because that's what I feel like right now. Dead. Or going to be, if I have to go through another consecutive night of forced baby-making.

Don't get me wrong, I love Graham. I love *being* with Graham. Any number of women would kill to be in my position. We've had quite a good run these last few years. It's just that when a plastic stick starts commanding you to do it on Monday, Tuesday, and Wednesday nights, all those passionate desires that you've spent the last few years blissfully indulging in start keeling over like dead ducks. Three nights in a row was a lot even on our honeymoon—and that was in Jamaica with the Bob Marley, and the rum punches, and no need to go to work the next day. Now, it's just a regular, chilly October in New England; and while I do love pumpkin spice lattes, they don't have quite the same *je ne sais quoi*.

This whole thing is so exhausting. I've peed on a stick for the fourth time this week, and I've gotten a smug little smiley face every single time. The smiley face is supposed to indicate that I'll ovulate within forty-eight hours. We're supposed to do it once or twice within those forty-eight hours, the smiley face is supposed to go away after my luteinizing hormones go back to whatever level they normally luteinize at, and then we're supposed to sit back, relax, and let the human reproductive system work its magic. Only, these tests appear to be malfunctioning. Or maybe *I'm* malfunctioning. Maybe I really *haven't* ovulated yet. And if I managed to miscalculate the release of the egg down the tube, there goes another month down the drain. The pressure is killing me.

I suppose Graham could be the one malfunctioning. We haven't explored that possibility yet. We're still just trying our best the old-fashioned way, since it hasn't been a full year yet. The doctors like to make you wait a year before sending you for fertility testing. It's close, though. Eleven months we've been trying. That's eleven disappointments, while everyone else we know is getting pregnant after their first or second try. Or, even worse, by accident.

By accident!

Sometimes I feel like running through the halls of the local high school, telling everyone to just go out and get pregnant now, while it's still easy! Yes, of course I know that's a terrible idea—particularly for a middle school librarian—and would ruin countless lives. But how unfair is it that during the most fertile time of your life, you're instructed to try your best to prevent it? And then, when you're ready for it to happen...sorry, too late. Well, too late for Graham and me. For all our friends and coworkers it's apparently the perfect time. Eternally fertile they are. Some of them already have two babies, when we haven't even managed to conjure up one. *Quality over quantity,* Graham always reminds me. Nice thought, but there isn't much quality in a nonexistent baby now is there?

I snap a photo of the ovulation stick and text it to Graham. It's late afternoon and I'm home from work. Graham is over at Eric's place, working on a new app. I want to give him some warning that our week of marathon lovemaking isn't quite done yet. There was an actual time in my life when the words *week of marathon lovemaking* and *Graham* would have had me completely hot and bothered. Now I'm just...bothered.

Graham replies within seconds.

Leaving soon. I'll bring the hard liquor. You put on that thing I like.

I laugh. We both know that the sexy lingerie phase went out the window months ago. Now, it's pretty much clothes off, under the blankets, down to business. *That thing I like* is code for the hooded sweatshirt and yoga pants I've been changing into the second I get home from work, ever since the weather turned cold.

He really is a good sport.

I feel slightly cheered as I come out of the bathroom and wander over to my underwear drawer. Even though I'd like nothing more than to lie on the couch and watch Buffy on Netflix, I suppose I could stand to spice things up a little. I pull out a lacy black bra and matching garter belt. I hold the garter belt up in the air and dangle the suspender clips around. Do I really want to put stockings on, too? And then have to shove all those clips into place? Last time I put them on I really wrenched my back. I sigh as I rifle around in the drawer. Do I even *have* stockings? I probably threw them out after the last time. Fingers crossed. No, wait. There they are. Darn it. Rolled up into two sad balls of fishnet, hiding behind my slipper socks. Now *those* would be nice to slip into.

I give the slipper socks one last, wistful look, before heading into the bathroom with a handful of lingerie. I'm about halfway dressed, freezing and covered in goose bumps, when I hear the front door open and close. Crap. How'd he get here so fast? I yank up the stockings, shove the clips haphazardly through the fabric, and dive onto the bed.

"I'm upstairs!" I yell, which is pretty obvious. It's not like I normally wait for him on the kitchen table. I definitely should have turned the heat up before I got into bed. It's *freezing* in here. I'm dying to get under the blankets, but the whole point of this is for Graham to actually see me looking attractive—not so he can hunt around for me inside a shivering mound of duvet. Finally, I hear him coming up the stairs. As the bedroom door opens, I stretch out across the bed. I shake my hair, arch my back—

"Oy, Summer!"

"Ahhhh!"

It's Mom. I just struck a seductive pose for *my mother*. I can't seem to stop screaming. I mean, why *would* I stop? What kind of a person would stop screaming in this situation? Not a sane one. I jump off the bed and wrap the duvet tightly around my body.

"How did you get in here?" I yell.

"I used my spare key!"

"That key is for emergencies! Why didn't you call first?"

"I did call! You didn't pick up!" She motions to the phone, which is flashing an orange message light.

"Well—" I pause. Having struck a seductive pose for my mother only moments ago, I'm finding it rather difficult to collect my thoughts. "You can't barge in here with your spare key, just because I didn't pick up the phone!"

Right! Now we're back in business.

"Well, I'm *sorry*," says Mom, in her *I'm so sorry for being your mother* voice of extreme guilt. "I only wanted to drop off the pants that I hemmed for you."

"What pants?" I snap.

"The black ones you were wearing yesterday. You looked like you were going to trip in them, so I took a few inches off."

Oh, God. I sink down on the bed, burying my face in my hands. Those pants were the perfect length for my work heels. Now I'll have to wear them with flats, and I hate wearing flats to work. Mom is obsessed with hemming my pants. I never ask her to do it because she turns them all into capris. But ever since Graham and I suffered a moment of temporary insanity, and bought a house three miles from my parents, Mom's been randomly popping in to do us favors.

"Can you please stop stealing my pants?" I mumble.

"What's all this about, anyway?" she asks, gesturing back and forth like she's scratching records at the club. It takes a second for me to realize that she's actually motioning between my head and the duvet that's wrapped around my body. "You *told* me to come up here. What's going on?"

"I was telling *Graham* to come up here, Mom. Not you. What do you *think* is going on?"

I watch as the energy efficient light bulb in Mom's head slowly goes from dim, to the full fifteen watts. Her cheeks redden with embarrassment, and she clamps one hand over her mouth. "At four o'clock on a Thursday?" she whispers and, despite everything that's happened, I have to fight back a giggle. She thinks this is normal behavior for us.

"You had kids," I say, giving her a meaningful look. "You should know how it works."

"You don't mean..."

"*Yes.*" I roll my eyes. "For a while now. Only...it hasn't been working. Obviously."

Man, this is uncomfortable. If you haven't noticed, Mom and

I don't exactly have that chummy, best-friendy sort of relationship that other mothers and daughters seem to enjoy. When I was in high school, we never shopped together or went for pedicures. We certainly never chatted about boys. And I had been under the comfortable impression that Hell would freeze over before we ever felt the need to talk about sex.

Yet, here we are.

This is actually the first time I've spoken to any of our family about the fact that we've been trying. I didn't want the added pressure of everybody knowing and always asking for updates. I didn't want to deal with everybody watching to see if I drank a glass of wine at family functions. We've always dodged the question of grandchildren by replying, "Maybe someday!" and leaving it at that.

But now, in the most awkward way possible, Mom has found out. And with that knowledge has come a look of total, maniacal ecstasy. It's as if I've told her that I'm already pregnant. With twins. She looks instantly younger—as if every concern she's ever had about leaving behind a legacy in this world has been erased. As if God himself has swooped down and proclaimed, *Joan shall have grandchildren! And they shall cure cancer!*

Grandchildren. Shiny, new humans to carry on the Hartwell genes. Mom hasn't looked this happy since the day she bought The Duffle. She looks as if she's hit the lottery and had an orgasm all at the same time, which is, frankly, disturbing. I'm relieved when her look of joy is quickly replaced by her more familiar look of complete and utter panic.

"Oy!" She turns around and heads for the door. "Let me get out of here before Graham gets home! The last thing he needs to find is his mother-in-law in his bedroom!"

She takes off down the stairs, faster than I've ever seen her move before, as if the lives of her future grandchildren are at stake. And, she may be right. The sight of his wife, dressed in lingerie, occupying the same room as Joan Eleanor Hartwell, might render Graham irreversibly impotent. I flop back on the pillows, as the front door slams shut.

I can't believe she hemmed my pants.

∼

BY THE TIME Graham gets home, I'm back in a hooded sweatshirt and yoga pants, lounging in bed watching Netflix. The good part is that after Mom left, I was inspired to go downstairs and pour myself a large glass of wine. The bad part is that said wine is causing me to nod off. I open one eye as Graham comes into the bedroom.

"I was *so* sexy earlier," I say, blowing my nose. I've also been having an allergy attack from Mom's perfume. "You should have seen me."

Graham raises his eyebrows as he takes off his watch. He places it on the nightstand and sits down on the bed next to me. "And...what happened?"

"Mom happened."

"Huh?"

"It's a long, disturbing story for another time," I say. "Here, I got you some wine." I reach across to the nightstand and hand Graham a glass.

"Thanks."

We sip our wine in silence for a few minutes, watching Buffy and Angel make out passionately onscreen.

"Is this, um...turning you on?" asks Graham.

"Not really. I'm just trying to finish season one."

"It's okay if it does," he says, shrugging. "I mean, I don't mind watching Sarah Michelle Gellar."

So, this is what it's come to. Graham and I watching *Buffy the Vampire Slayer* as foreplay. I turn off Netflix.

"What?"

"Let's just do this," I say, attempting to pull my sweatshirt over my head. I took my contact lenses out earlier, due to the allergy attack, and now the sweatshirt doesn't want to fit over my eyeglasses. I carefully stretch the neck hole out as far as it will go, easing it over my head, and knocking my glasses askew. My hair crackles with static. I straighten out my glasses and smooth down my hair. Victoria's Secret models have nothing on me.

Graham stares at me, but not in a good way.

"What?"

"You're like an onion," he says, motioning to the long-sleeve shirt that I'm still wearing.

"Think of it like a striptease," I say. "Now it's your turn."

He takes off his shirt. There is, of course, nothing under it. "Done."

I roll my eyes and pull off my long-sleeve shirt. At the sight of the tank top underneath, we both start to laugh. "Last layer, I *swear*. Can we get under the covers now?"

"We haven't done pants!"

Graham jumps off the bed and removes his jeans. He's wearing red, white, and blue Fourth of July boxers. I pull off my yoga pants, revealing a pair of leggings underneath. So much for sneaking those off unnoticed.

"You're ridiculous," he laughs, joining me back in bed. I put my glasses on the nightstand and roll onto my side so that we're facing each other. Graham pulls me into his chest until I've warmed up.

"I was reading the message boards today," I say, after things have progressed past the point of bringing up the subject of Internet message boards. Still, this is important.

"Oh, yeah?" says Graham, stopping what he was doing and propping himself up on an elbow. I can tell he's annoyed. He hates when I get on the mommy boards. I read every bit of fertility advice, dating back the last ten years, and every day I find something new, or something that we haven't tried yet, or something that I've been doing wrong. There's *always* something that I've been doing wrong.

"Yeah. I was reading that a lot of women are using egg whites as...you know...lubricant."

"*Egg whites?*"

"Yeah."

"Like, raw egg whites?"

"Yeah."

Graham is now sitting up all the way. "You're saying you want me to crack an egg down there?" He points under the covers, looking genuinely horrified. As he very well should.

"*You* don't have to do it," I say. "I would. I'd do it in the kitchen, obviously. Then I'd...like...put them into a syringe."

I cringe as I hear the words out loud. They sounded so much more scientific and reasonable when they were safely inside my head. Now, I'm forced to actually picture myself holding a syringe and a carton of Eggland's Best.

"You've completely lost your mind," says Graham, raking his hands through his hair and sending it into a million different directions. "This is *raw egg* we're talking about, Summer. With salmonella. There's a reason your mother never let you eat raw cookie dough, and it's not just because she's nuts."

"Okay, *fine*," I say, rolling over in a huff. "It was just a thought."

"You have to get off those websites."

"That's easy for you to say! You've got one job to do! I'm the one who has to worry about egg whites, and holding my legs in the air, and piercing my nostrils."

"Oh, Summer."

"I'm not going to do it!" I sort of scream. "I just heard that it increases blood flow to the uterus."

"From your *nostrils*?"

"Just forget it, okay?"

Graham sighs. "Look, I know this is hard. But it's going to happen without all these crazy tricks. And we don't have to do it tonight if you don't want to. We've already put in a good effort this month."

I close my eyes. "I guess."

"You know, they say that when you stop trying, that's when it happens."

"That's what people who get pregnant by accident say."

He doesn't respond for a moment, probably because he knows I'm right.

"I think they just mean that we should try to relax," he says, finally. He snuggles down next to me, stroking my hair as we listen to the wind whistling outside. Even though I'm totally stressed out, this is pretty nice.

"I could always get something pierced," says Graham. "If you think it would help."

I laugh. "Please don't."

"Yeah, your dad might try to copy me."

"Gross!" I shudder. "Now we definitely need to call it a night."

"That reminds me." Graham jumps out of bed, picks his jeans up off the floor, and rifles around in the pockets. "I got you something today." He jumps back into bed and holds a box in front of my face.

"What's this?"

"Open it."

Inside the box is an opaque pink stone, surrounded by tiny diamonds, hanging from a long, silver chain.

"It's a fertility necklace," says Graham.

I burst out laughing. "You're kidding?"

"What? It's better than egg whites and nostril piercings. It's rose quartz. I read that it reduces stress and acts as an aphrodisiac."

"You were on the mommy boards!" I gently punch him in the stomach.

"I call it Google."

"You're as crazy as I am," I laugh. "But, I love it. Thank you."

I sit up and hold my hair aside while Graham fastens the chain around my neck. When he's finished, he slides his hands around my waist and kisses down the side of my neck. The goose bumps are back. Only this time, I'm not cold. I turn my face slightly toward his.

"Once more, for luck?" I ask.

"I suppose we ought to try it out."

So we do.

THREE MONTHS

2

"Mine were natural," says Linda. "All three. I can't believe that anyone who loves their children would get an epidural. I mean, you're basically injecting *drugs* directly into your child's body. What kind of a woman would *do* that?"

I sit quietly across the lunch table, nodding and eating grapes. I had been happily eating baby carrots until Linda told me that baby carrots are made from deformed full-sized carrots and soaked in chlorine. Then she made me throw them away. Now, all I have left are these grapes, which I lied and said were organic. They're not. I got three pounds of them for seven bucks at Costco. But I'm too scared of Linda to be honest with her. She's had three children—all at home, all epidural-free, and all videotaped by her father-in-law. Barf. When the time comes, I can't imagine wanting John anywhere near the delivery room, never mind pointing a video camera between my legs.

Let me back up a bit.

I'm pregnant!

I can't say for sure which of those four nights, back in October, was the one that did the trick, but I'm nearly three months along now! I like to think it was the last night that we tried—the night when we almost gave up, but didn't. The night that Graham just so happened to wrap a fertility stone around my neck. And because of that last ditch effort, there is now a tiny baby Blenderman growing inside of me, causing me to vomit every single morning and twice on Tuesday. Twice on Monday, too, if I remember correctly.

Ever since I told the girls at work, our lunch breaks have been nothing but baby talk. Meaning, we talk about baby stuff. We don't talk to each other in baby voices, although that might be preferable to some of the weird things that have come out of Linda's mouth. The few male teachers that used to eat with us have all mysteriously started eating at their desks.

"So, what I did," continues Linda, digging her fork into her homemade farro salad, "was have her insert it into capsules that I take like a vitamin." She takes a bite of salad and washes it down with some sort of green, chunky juice inside a mason jar. Leaves are floating at the bottom. She might actually be drinking the stuff that Mom used to scrape out of our fish tank.

"Excuse me?" I ask.

I missed some important detail when my mind started wandering. I don't actually want to know what she's been talking about, but if I appear confused she'll make me another jug of Dragon's Blood tea—used to treat tuberculosis, parasites, and Alzheimer's disease—and I'd hate to have to pour another gallon of that stuff down the drain.

"My placenta," says Linda, pointing her fork at me. "I had my doula steam it and put it into capsules. I still take them every month during my period."

And...lunch is over. I spit half a grape out of my mouth, and start packing up my lunch bag. "I think I'm going to go back to the library. I have a lot of books to shelve before next, um...period."

"Okay," says Linda. "Let me know if you want to borrow that recipe book."

"Will do."

I so will not. Linda's latest craze is packing her husband and children bento boxes for lunch every day. She crafts caterpillars and exotic birds out of raisins, celery, and rice. I didn't even realize that packing your husband a lunch was a *thing*. I know Mom always did it for Dad, but I just assumed it was because she treated him like a child.

Note to self: Ask Graham what the heck he's been eating for lunch.

"I'll come with you," says Rachel, gathering up her things and following me out of the teacher's lounge. Rachel is also pregnant, but four months ahead of me—a fact that she is constantly flaunting. She's always making these vague references about what's to come. As if she doesn't want to give away too much information and spoil the surprise. *Just wait until you have the glucose test,* she told me with a knowing smile. *Just wait until you watch the C-section video in childbirth class.* News flash, Rach. I can watch a C-section video any time I want to on YouTube. But I don't. And guess what? I'm not going to watch the one in childbirth class either. I don't need to see what's going to happen on the other side of the curtain. That's why there's a curtain.

"Placenta capsules," I say, as we walk down the corridor. "Can you believe her?"

"I *know*," says Rachel. "Totally gross. Although, it might be a good idea?"

She looks at me questioningly. Even though we make fun of Linda, I know that Rachel really looks up to her. While I try my best—and often fail—to filter the actual important information from the barrage of fads and scare tactics that one is hit with daily when pregnant, Rachel laps all of it up. And, I'll admit, she's quite good at getting inside my head.

"You're considering it?" I ask, crinkling up my nose. When Linda said it, a mere five minutes ago, I was so certain that it was weird and gross and never going to happen. But now, five minutes later, the thought, *I wonder if I can order them online,* has scrolled across my mind. No. They can't possibly be available online. That would mean I'd have to mail my placenta off somewhere. Do they even let you take it home from the hospital? It would probably need to be packed in ice. I picture us walking out of the hospital, carrying a car seat and an Igloo cooler marked *Biohazard.*

Rachel shrugs. "I don't know. You never know with these things. Better safe than sorry, right? Oh, that reminds me. Are you banking the baby's cord blood?"

"Cord blood?"

"In case they ever need the stem cells."

"Stem cells?"

"I forgot you're only three months along," she says, smiling. "They'll tell you all about it in childbirth class. You've got plenty of time. Not like me." She rolls her eyes and pats her large stomach. "I'll catch you later."

Rachel pops back into her sixth grade classroom, and I continue along alone to the library. As I start re-shelving library books, I can't get thoughts of placenta capsules out of my head. Is this really something that a lot of people do? I've got to check the mommy boards. I glance longingly at the computer on my desk. If I didn't have a class of seventh graders coming in soon, I'd be on there right now. Not that I want the school IT guy to know I've been researching ways to eat my own internal organs. Maybe I should wait until I get home.

What if Linda's right, though? What if they're super nutritious and the only way I'll get back to full health after giving birth? What if I don't take them and I turn into this anemic wraith of a woman, while Rachel's over there pumping iron like She-Ra? It's not fair. You never think about this stuff before you get pregnant. You think about cuddly babies, and cute outfits, and registering for crib bedding. Then you get pregnant and it's like you're on *The Walking Dead*.

I picture Linda as a zombie, and I laugh out loud just as my students come filing in.

"What's so funny, Mrs. B?" asks one of the boys.

"Oh, nothing," I say. "Just this book." I grab a random one off the cart. *A History of World War II*. The kid looks at me as if I've lost it.

If he only knew.

~

"How are you feeeeeling?" asks Tanya in a singsong voice. She's doing this goofy, Tweedledee sort of a walk as she comes toward me, hands outstretched to touch my stomach. She and Eric claim that they never want to have children. But the way she's been acting around me lately makes me wonder. Mom would certainly be thrilled if they changed their minds. As much as she loves Graham, he's not going to carry on the Hartwell name.

"I'm good," I say. "Really good."

"Any weird cravings yet?"

"Um, not really. Yesterday I tried pomegranate for the first time. Does that count?"

She squeals in delight and claps her hands. I can't imagine the mayhem if I ever attempt pickles and ice cream.

"HOW ARE YOU?" shouts Mom, who seems to think pregnancy causes hearing loss. She hip-checks Graham out of the way, and gets right up close to my face. "COME SIT! LET ME

BRING YOU SOMETHING TO DRINK!" She leads me into the dining room, where I see that she's dragged an upholstered wingback chair in from the living room.

"You really didn't need to do this," I say, as she pushes me into it. "I'm fine in a regular chair."

"Oh, no!" says Mom, pointing her finger at me. "We don't want your sciatica flaring up!"

"Since when do I get sciatica?"

Ignoring me, Mom plunks a glass of orange juice on the table. "DRINK."

"Orange juice? With dinner?" I crinkle my nose.

"It has plenty of pulp," she says, as if that fact has ever made anything better. "The baby needs fiber." As soon as Mom goes back into the kitchen, Graham chugs the juice for me. I hate pulp.

We're all gathered at my parents' house for our monthly Friday night dinner. Once Graham and I sold our condo in Boston and moved closer to my childhood—okay, fine, *early adulthood*—home, Mom and Dad decided to start this family tradition. It's all very *Gilmore Girls*. Eric and Tanya are still living in Boston, so it's a bit of a drive for them. But it's worth it. We've actually been having a pretty good time when all of us get together. Take last month's dinner. Dad took out this old video of Eric trying to ice skate, with his legs shooting out in every direction, and we all just about died laughing. Except for Eric. Which is, of course, what made it so funny.

"Richard!" shouts Mom from the kitchen. "Come help with the roast! I need to put out the salads!"

Dad, who had been sitting at the dining room table, happily sipping a Manhattan, heads obediently into the kitchen to rev up the electric carving knife. That knife has always seemed like a disaster waiting to happen. Every memory I have of Thanksgiving at our house is mingled with the sound of that carving knife, followed by the smell of burning motor oil. As Dad sets to work, Mom parades salad bowls out of the kitchen and places one in front of each of us. Lettuce, tomato, cucumber. No onions. Onions give stomachaches. Canned green beans on the side. Totally unseasoned roast beef. The Hartwells don't do spices. They do a hunk of beef, popped into the oven, and sliced up by Richard "Jason Voorhees" Hartwell.

Still, while the food may be plain, there's something comforting about the predictability of it all. I actually *like* coming here on Fridays and spending time with my family. You know, just as long as I get to go home at the end of the night.

"HOW WAS WORK TODAY?" screams Mom, when we're all finally settled in. Dad is still in possession of his fingers for another week.

"You know, you don't have to shout," I say. "It might hurt the baby's ears." I don't think the baby even has ears at this point, but saying that should tone Mom down a little. She puts her fingers guiltily over her mouth.

"*How was work today?*" she whispers.

"*It was fine,*" I whisper back. "The usual. Dewey decimal system this, Internet research that." I leave out the part about my own bit of Internet research. Placenta capsules. Yuck. One quick Google image search was enough to tell me that I will never be ingesting those things. Ever. My stomach turns as I stab into a tomato.

"You must be tired," says Mom. "Having to work all day."

I shrug. "I'm used to it."

"It'll be nice though, when you don't have to work anymore."

"Right," I laugh. "Only thirty more years."

"I mean, after you have the baby."

"Oh, right," I say. "It's kind of too bad, though, that it's going to be a summer baby. Most of my maternity leave will wind up being over summer vacation."

Mom's fork clatters onto her plate. "What are you talking about?"

"Um, I'm having the baby in July. I get eight weeks' maternity leave. That means I'll have to go back to work shortly after school starts in September."

Mom's just staring at me, bug-eyed. I wipe my mouth with a napkin and look nervously around the table. "What?"

"You're not seriously considering going back to work?"

"Of course I am. Why not?"

"Your husband is a millionaire!"

"Most of it's tied up in stocks, actually," chimes in Graham.

"That's none of their business," I say, giving him a look. "And also not the point. I love my job. I'm not just going to give up my career because I had a baby!"

"Oy, Richard! She wants to go back to work after the baby comes!"

"If she wants to go back to work, she should go back to work." Dad shrugs and takes a large bite of roast beef.

"Thank you," I say.

Mom shoots daggers at him, but he doesn't seem to notice. Don't bother trying to talk to Dad on roast beef night. He's forking in the green beans like he's just been released from prison.

"Well, who's going to watch the baby?" she asks, throwing her arms in the air.

I kick Graham under the table.

"We're going to put the little tyke into day care," says Graham, cheerfully. "Building Blocks Learning Academy. It's right near Summer's school. Easy drop-off, easy pickup. Great reviews on Yelp."

"Yelp," repeats Mom, the color draining from her face.

"Oh, I've read about that place!" says Tanya. "They focus on the *whole* child." I give her a strange look and she shrugs.

"Day care," murmurs Mom. "I feel faint." She slumps back into her chair with one hand across her forehead. Dad reluctantly puts down his fork, stands up, and pulls Mom's chair away from the table. He lifts her feet onto his now empty chair. This is sort of how I always pictured this conversation going, to be honest.

"Look, Mom," I say. "Day care is fine. Everybody does it, and most kids turn out just fine."

"Most kids!"

"*All* kids. I mean to say *all* kids." I look pleadingly at Graham. What did I have to go and say *most* for? The Hartwell anxiety is strong in me. "*All* kids are fine at day care, right Graham?"

"Of course," he says. "Only like, six percent turn out to be murderers." I kick him hard, underneath the table.

"You're digging my grave," says Mom, weakly.

"Excuse me?"

"Shovel by shovel. You're digging my grave."

I roll my eyes. "You're being a little dramatic."

Mom's eyes fly open. Either she's regaining consciousness or she's been possessed by Zuul. "NO GRANDCHILD OF MINE WILL GO TO DAY CARE!"

There is no Joan, only Zuul! Crikey.

"Okay," I say, slowly. "Take it easy. Let's just pretend for a minute that this isn't 1950, and that I have the right to go back to work if I want to. What do *you* suggest we do with the baby?" I don't like the way this conversation is headed.

"Mom and Dad could watch the baby," says Eric. "They're retired. What else are they going to do with their lives?"

And just like that, Mom's spirit is funneled back into her limp body. Zuul has gone. She jumps out of the chair, her face glowing.

"We can watch the baby!" she says. "We'll come to your

house! Every day we'll come to your house and babysit until you get home from work!"

"Every day?" asks Dad, looking concerned. "But Joan, what about our plans?"

"What plans?" Mom looks at him as if she's never seen him before in her life.

"Like, going out to lunch," he says. "And...and breakfast."

"Oy, please." Mom bats a hand at him. "When the baby's old enough, we'll bring him with us."

Dad doesn't look so sure about this. I don't feel so sure about this either. Not only are they suddenly babysitting my child on a daily basis—overdressing him, overprotecting him, following old-school parenting advice from the doctors who thought it was cool to smoke Camels—but they're going to be carting him around in their car? I've seen Dad try to parallel park in his old age. It's frightening, to say the least.

"It'll save you so much money," says Mom. "Why should you waste so much money?"

"Five minutes ago you said my husband was a millionaire."

Mom ignores me. "You simply can't put a two-month-old child into daycare, with the germs and the choking. It's settled. If you insist on going back to work"—and on that point, she lets out a maniacal laugh— "then *we're* going to watch the baby." She slaps her hand on the table, sending all the plates into a synchronized leap, and indicating an end to the conversation. She starts jauntily clearing away plates, while Dad follows her into the kitchen, asking questions about how all of this will affect his retirement.

I slump back in my chair, looking around at my remaining family members. "What just happened?"

Tanya reaches over and squeezes my hand. "You have to admit that it makes sense, Sum. You've got two loving parents, close by, who want to take care of your baby. You're *lucky*."

"Lucky." I kick the word around in my head for a few seconds, before focusing my wrath on Eric. "You just had to open your big mouth, didn't you?"

"Oh, come on. You think she hadn't already thought of this? If you ask me, she was *hoping* you'd decide to go back to work."

Oh, God. He's probably right. I look at Graham. "And what about you? Do you think this is a good idea?"

"I'm not going to say that Richard and Joan molding my child into an overanxious germaphobe is a good idea." He takes a sip of wine. "But it's a *nice* idea. We should probably give them the chance to bond. I mean, my parents are in Florida. Richard and Joan are the only grandparents the baby is going to have around for most of the year."

"We could get a nanny," I say. "The baby could bond with the nanny."

"That would crush them," says Tanya. "It's too late for that."

She's right. And as much as I want to blame this on Eric's big mouth, I know the idea has to have been lurking around Mom's head for months. Probably years.

"Okay, fine," I say. "We'll give them a chance. But they're not allowed to drive the baby in their car. And I still want to do day care, eventually. I want the baby to be socialized. I don't want him having nobody but Grandma and Grandpa for friends."

"Having flashbacks to high school, eh, Sum?" asks Eric.

I kick him hard, underneath the table.

FIVE MONTHS

3

"Trust me," says Mom, tugging at the back of my shirt. "Nobody's going to be looking at your ass anymore."

"What's *that* supposed to mean?"

We're in a changing room at JC Penney, surrounded by discarded items of hideous maternity wear—the item of hideous maternity wear currently shrouding my body, not long for this world.

"You're *pregnant*, Summer. You're going to have a huge stomach. Nobody's going to be checking out your ass." Mom makes *huge stomach* motions with her hands, and then gestures flippantly to my rear end. She's turning into quite the foul-mouthed little mime in her old age.

"Do you mean that nobody's going to *notice* my ass because my stomach will be so huge?" I ask. "Or do you mean that my ass is going to become so huge and revolting that nobody, including my own husband, will want to look at it anymore?"

"Oy, please," says Mom, batting a hand at me. "Graham's a good boy. He's not going anywhere."

True. But, still. I wasn't planning on ballooning up ten sizes and completely giving up on my appearance.

"I still don't want to look frumpy," I say. "Not just for Graham, but for myself. When you look good, you feel good. Haven't you heard that before?"

Mom stops fussing with the back of my shirt and looks at me seriously in the mirror. "Don't tell me you want to be like one of those hot moms?"

Hot moms. That's what Mom calls anyone who puts effort into her appearance—for example, a mother who wears shoes not manufactured at the New Balance factory. To Mom, the only thing worse than being a hot mom is being a meth addict, and I'm pretty sure she thinks that both of them should have their children taken away. I'm also pretty sure that by seven months she expects me to have stopped shaving and wearing deodorant.

"So what if I do?" I ask. "What's so bad about being a hot mom, anyway? Why do you always have to equate looking good with being a bad mother? It doesn't make any sense. Am I required to be frumpy in order to earn your respect? Is that what you're telling me? From here on out it's Frump City or I'm out of the family?"

Somewhat hysterically, I wrench the back of my shirt out of her hand and turn to inspect my butt in the mirror. I'm wearing the world's most heinous pair of maternity jeans. The waist part fits okay, since it's made from a giant rubber band. But the butt is just this loose, sad sack of fabric. It's not even really denim. These aren't even really jeans. They're chambray. Oh, God. I'm wearing acid wash chambray maternity pants with a rubber band waist. My face crumples.

"That's not what I *said*, Summer. I just don't think that a mother should be so concerned with her own appearance. Once the baby comes, he or she is going to be your first priority."

"*Obviously*. But I'm still going to need to put a pair of pants on in the morning. Why does it matter if they're tight instead of baggy?" I grab a fistful of chambray and shake it at her.

"But don't you want to be comfortable?" asks Mom, stripping away all philosophical debate and getting right down to her basic point: *Big pants comfy.*

"Well, yeah," I say. "But nice-looking pants can be comfortable too."

Mom frowns. "Would it help if I took them up a few inches?" She squats down beside me and starts turning up the hem of the pants, exposing my ankles and striped socks. I look like a Dr. Seuss character. I jerk my leg out of her grasp and sink down onto the bench, burying my face in my hands. It's not unusual for a shopping trip with my mother to end in tears of frustration. Just imagine the joy of trying to do it with pregnancy hormones.

Mom sighs and stands up. "How about this?"

I look up to see her waving around a blue and white floral top with a ribbon around the waist.

"Where did you get that? I *never* picked that."

"It was already in here," says Mom. "There's a lot of good stuff already in here." She rifles through a hook overflowing with shapeless, flowery dresses. I never realized that eighty-year-old women were in such need of maternity clothes.

I stand up and pluck the shirt out of her hand. "This stuff was left behind for a reason." I usher her out of the changing room, lock the door with a satisfying thunk, and remove the chambray pants. I pull on the black leggings that I wore this morning and take a deep breath, rubbing my hands over my stomach.

I'd be perfectly happy wearing leggings for the next four months. The problem is, as soon as Mom found out that I was pregnant, she started doing the weirdest thing. She started going maternity clothes shopping with *Dad*. She'd make him chauffeur her around to places like Babies R Us and Motherhood Maternity, and then he'd follow her around the store, carrying her pocketbook and all the clothes that she picked out. One time, the store clerk asked him when his wife was due. Then they'd stop by our house with bags of clearance rack maternity clothing, guaranteed to ensure that I never become pregnant again.

I figured the only way to make it stop was to offer to take Dad's place. My hope is that Mom will realize my tastes and her tastes are nothing alike, and that perhaps maternity clothes shopping should be my own responsibility. So far, no luck. She seems to really enjoy dressing me up and pointing out the order in which my looks are going to fade.

I dump everything on the rack outside the fitting room, except for a pair of white capri pants that will look really cute with some wedge heels. Not that I have any intention of wearing wedge heels, but it was worth saying it just to see the look on Mom's face. She fingers the fabric distastefully as the clerk rings them up.

"So, where do you want to eat lunch?" I ask.

"What kind of underwear are you going to wear with these?" she asks loudly, pulling the pants out of the bag and stretching the hips apart. "They're practically see-through!"

The only thing that could make Mom forget about lunch is the possibility of her only daughter being five months pregnant and wearing see-through pants.

"A thong," I say.

"Oy!"

"What?"

"I wear Hanes," she whispers. "Full coverage." She makes *full coverage* motions with her hands, implying that her underwear comes to within the vicinity of her rib cage.

"That's great, Mom."

"I thought you said you wanted to be comfortable? We could go look for some briefs." She points back into the depths of JC Penney.

"You know what would make me really comfortable?"

"What?"

"Never talking to you about my underwear ever again." I take her by the elbow and lead her out of JC Penney, pointing her in the direction of the food court. "Let's go eat."

"If it's a boy, what do you think about the name Benjamin?" asks Mom, once we're settled in the food court with two trays of French fries and Whoppers spread out before us. I'll admit that this was half the reason I agreed to come to the mall today.

I shrug. "It's not bad. Hey, I meant to tell you that we're thinking about using Richard for a middle name. After Dad."

Instead of the look of gratitude I was expecting, Mom looks as if I've slapped her.

"What? What did I say?"

"That sort of thing just isn't *done* in the Jewish tradition," says Mom.

"Oh. Why not?"

"You don't name babies after living relatives," she explains, dunking a French fry into ketchup. "It's bad luck. It's like you're just *waiting* for that relative to die."

"It's not like that at all!" I protest. "I thought it would be *nice*. I thought Dad would be honored."

"Your father would be horrified," says Mom. "And devastated."

"*Okay*, geez. I'm sorry. How about Randy?"

Mom puts her Whopper down on the tray. "Randy?"

"Yeah. Like Randy Travis or Randy Jackson?" Mom loves *American Idol.*

"Listen to me, Summer. You have to think about how the name will sound when the baby is a grown-up. You have to test it out by putting *Mister* in front of it."

"Mister Randy? What is he, a kindergarten teacher?"

Mom gives me a stern look. "I just don't think it sounds very mature. What about a nice, classic name like David? Or Michael?"

"You think Mister Michael sounds better than Mister Randy?"

"Yes. I do."

I roll my eyes. "How about Mistoffelees?"

"Who?"

"Mister Mistoffelees."

Mom glares at me. "This is serious, Summer. You can't name your child Mister Mistoffelees."

"You *really* think we're going to name him that?"

She shrugs. That's how much faith she has in my decision-making abilities.

I shrug back. "Mister Randy Richard Mistoffelees Blenderman. You'd better start thinking up nicknames. How do you feel about Dick?"

We look stubbornly at each other for a few seconds. And then, in an unprecedented, very un-Mom-like move, she picks up a French fry and whips it at my forehead. In another unprecedented move, we both start to laugh.

I blame the hormones.

~

GRAHAM and I stare at the aisles of walkers, bouncers, jumpers, and swings, our heads turning left and right, like we're watching a tennis match.

"So...which ones do we actually need?" I ask, swallowing hard.

Graham looks at me. "You think *I* know?"

I shrug. The scanner hangs limply by my side as I nervously click the buttons.

"Stop doing that," says Graham, pulling the scanner out of

my hand. "You're probably registering for all kinds of stuff by mistake."

"What could I possibly be registering for right now?" I ask. "The floor? My shoes? Do you see a bar code on that piece of gum?"

"No," he says, peering into the little screen. "But I think you may have deleted the diaper cream."

I let out a small moan. "That was a third of our registry!"

We've been here over an hour, and registered for three items. Needless to say, we're both quite tense at the moment. As soon as Mom and I came home from clothes shopping, Graham and I headed out to Babies R Us to start registering for the baby shower. *How hard can it be?* we thought. Obviously we've never been inside a Babies R Us before.

It's just…monstrous.

"This one looks fun," says Graham, pointing to a walker that's been left in the middle of the aisle. It looks like a yellow sports car. Figures. "Test it out."

I walk over and roll it back and forth a few times.

"Not like *that*."

"What?"

"Like this." Graham steps into the walker, jamming his feet through holes intended to fit a seven-month-old baby's thighs. He gets in up to his shins, and starts trudging down the aisle.

"Beep! Beep!"

"Oh, geez." I cover my face with my hands.

"Get the clicker, Sum. This one's a winner!"

I quickly scan the bar code just to make him stop. "Do we even *need* one of these?"

"Sure we do," he says. "Now, try this one." He shoves another big, round plastic contraption toward me. It's covered in jungle animals. I look around to make sure the coast is clear, then I put my feet through the holes. I flick a butterfly on a spring, making it bob back and forth.

"Fun?"

"This is stupid."

"You didn't choose the most stimulating of the activities. Try the bongos." He shuffles over to demonstrate, but the edge of his walker hits the edge of my contraption, and he can't reach.

"You're going to get us kicked out of here," I laugh.

"All part of my plan," says Graham, giving me a wink. "But maybe we should take a break."

He nearly falls over extricating his feet from the walker. Then he helps me out of mine, and we head to the nursery furniture section. We sit down in two gliders and put our feet up. This is nice. Much better than wandering up and down the aisles asking each other if we need a Travel System with SafeMax or a Travel System with SnugRide, or perhaps the Lux Travel System with LiteMax. Why can't the baby be light and snug *and* safe? It's all so overwhelming. I'm pretty sure when I was a baby Mom just stuck me in a wicker basket and slid me into the backseat.

"Maybe we should have brought someone more knowledgeable along," I say, picturing Linda from work. Yeah, right. She'd be horrified if she knew we were at Babies R Us. She'd tell me that everything here is made out of poisonous materials and make me register at some Etsy shop. She probably doesn't even own a car seat because she just bikes her kids everywhere.

"We're fine," says Graham. "We'll give it one more hour, then we'll go get Mexican."

"Okay," I say, my stomach growling at the thought of tacos. I lean my head against the glider and close my eyes.

"Summer?"

My eyes fly open. It's Rachel from work, standing in the aisle with her husband, Josh, who looks as if he's being walked to the gallows.

"Oh. Hey, Rachel," I say, sitting up a bit. "What are you guys doing here?"

She points to the shopping cart. "Just getting the rest of the stuff off my registry. I didn't get *any* of the breast-feeding equipment that I needed." She rolls her eyes. "Have you picked out your pump yet?"

Your pump. As if it's only a matter of choosing which one. As if there's no alternative. I chew on my lip, unsure of what to say. Do I tell her that the thought of breast-feeding keeps me up at night? I mean, I'd like to try it. I guess. Actually, no I wouldn't. I feel *obligated* to try it. In reality, the idea has never appealed to me. Does that make me a bad person? All the pressure to do it makes me feel so guilty. Like, as a consequence of my selfishness, my child is going to have a low IQ, and allergies, and acid reflux for life. Not that I necessarily believe all that. I just feel so judged. And, to be honest, ashamed. I feel ashamed of the fact that I'm not dying to do it.

Add it to the list.

"Not yet," I say. "But we're heading there next!" I smile at Graham who gives me a strange look. We've already talked about this subject extensively.

"I went with the double pump," says Rachel. "Anyway, after this we're going to a specialty shop in Newton where they sell handwoven diapers soaked in coconut and argan oil. I got the name from Linda."

I giggle. "You're going to buy wet diapers?"

"They're dry," she says, like I'm a moron. "They've just been infused with natural moisturizers. You can't trust the diaper creams they sell at these places."

"But what happens when you wash them?" I ask. "Don't all the oils come out?"

"You have to scrub them by hand with a special brush and soap. Then you hang them to dry."

"Do you really think you're going to have time to be hand-washing and air-drying diapers?" I ask, crinkling my nose.

"It doesn't matter what *I* want, Summer. It's all about the *baby* now. If we can't make a small sacrifice like this, what kind of mothers are we going to be?" She looks at Josh and laughs. He doesn't crack a smile. I'm guessing he's figured out who the one scrubbing all the diapers is going to be.

Still. I feel a bit thrown. I'd been planning to zap a few boxes of Pampers onto the registry; it was the one thing I thought I had figured out. Diapers: they catch the poo. Simple enough. Now, I have to worry about my baby's butt turning into an un-moisturized disaster due to my selfish behavior? Once again, it's Summer with the selfish behavior. First, with the hot mom outfits and the name Randy, and now with the breastfeeding and the unwillingness to hand-wash diapers. Maybe the universe is trying to tell me something. Maybe the universe is looking around at all the pregnant women thinking, *How'd we let this one slip through?*

"Well, it was great seeing you!" says Rachel, completely unaware of the inner turmoil she's inflicted upon me. "I'll see you at work on Monday."

"Yeah. See ya." I slump back into the glider and turn to Graham. "Do we have time to go to the coconut diaper store?"

"You're not serious?" asks Graham.

"I might be," I say. "I mean, why should Rachel's baby have a healthy, naturally moisturized butt, while ours has a rashy one all slathered in chemicals?"

"The diaper cream we picked is *fine*. It has Lightning McQueen on the box."

"Oh, God." I bury my face in my hands. "What were we

thinking? It's bad enough that I don't want to breastfeed. Now I can't even be bothered to hand-wash a few diapers?"

"We're not back to breast-feeding again, are we?"

"Everyone is dying to do it except for me," I mumble.

"You read breast-feeding message boards, Summer. Of course the people on there are dying to do it."

"What about Rachel?"

"Rachel does whatever Linda tells her to do. You're not like that. You form your own opinions."

"But my own opinions make me feel terrible," I say. "I feel like I'm this cold and horrible person. Do you think I'm a cold and horrible person?"

Graham stands up and walks over, crouching down in front of my glider.

"Do you think that I would have a baby with a cold and horrible person?"

I shrug. "Maybe you didn't know the real me until I got pregnant. Now it's too late."

He makes a face. "You mean that's not just because of the pregnancy hormones?"

I whack him in the chest.

"I'm joking," he continues. "I wanted this. With *you*. You're a warm and loving person, and you're going to be a warm and loving mother. Even warm and loving mothers are allowed to make selfish choices sometimes. That's what keeps them from becoming miserable and resentful mothers. They make formula for a reason, you know?"

"Yeah, for the people who try to breast-feed but can't. The magazine articles don't even *mention* the ones who don't want to do it at all. It's like it's too shameful a state of mind to even admit it exists."

"My mother didn't breast-feed me," says Graham. "And look how I turned out."

I groan.

"Look, Sum. It's not for everyone. Nothing is. I'm sure there are plenty of women like you. They're all just hiding in the shadows because they're afraid of being judged by the Lindas of the world. It doesn't mean that there's anything *wrong* with you. Okay?"

I roll my eyes.

"*Okay?*"

"Okay," I mumble.

"Good. Now, let's finish zapping stuff. I think I saw some formula with Ronald McDonald on the can."

"Perfect," I say, as he heaves me out of the glider. "Maybe later we can stop at The Home Depot for some sandpaper. I'm thinking about just making my own diapers."

"We're going to be such awesome parents," he says, squeezing my hand as we head back into the abyss.

SEVEN MONTHS

4

It's an odd thing, all your relatives guessing how large your stomach has become. I don't think it would ever be deemed appropriate to play such a game at the expense of, say, Graham's Uncle Chuck. Yet, there's Chuck, happily measuring out a piece of yarn large enough to wrap around Jupiter, and I'm just supposed to sit back and *enjoy* it? At least my stomach has a baby inside of it. God knows what's inside Uncle Chuck's. Three quarters of the brunch buffet, if you ask me.

I'm a bit crabby, I know. I'm just so tired all the time now. I do one thing per day and I'm *done*. At work I pretty much wheel myself around in my desk chair. I've started using the elevator. I'm in bed at seven p.m. and I haven't had a decent bowel movement in over a week. I get these terrible Braxton Hicks contractions where my stomach turns hard as a rock. I've just had it. I had it before arriving at my baby shower, and I've most definitely had it with this humiliating game. I fork a large chunk of cake into my mouth and glare at Uncle Chuck.

"Time's up!" announces Tanya. She walks around the room collecting everybody's piece of yarn. Dad's cut his absurdly short, but I appreciate the gesture. Graham, the gentleman that he is, refused to play. Everybody else can bite me. There are so many guests that by the time Tanya is done, she looks like she's holding a pom-pom. I try to stand still while she wraps each piece of yarn around my middle, making disapproving sounds when each one comes up short.

"Just wait until I do this to *you* someday," I whisper.

"Not likely," she whispers back. "Although, we've been thinking about adopting."

"No way! That's awesome!"

"Yeah, we were thinking one, or maybe even two. I've always wanted to get—" We're interrupted by a loud cheer from the bar. The Red Sox are winning.

I told Mom not to invite so many people. I told her that half the people on her guest list would be much happier if they could just stay home and watch the Red Sox game—a point that has just been proven. But Mom decided that since the Florida wedding had such a small guest list, the baby shower should attempt to make up for it. Apparently one of Dad's third cousins was offended that she missed out on nearly falling into a sinkhole. Since I will never be forgiven for planning the wedding without Mom, I chose not to push the issue. So, here we are at the Holiday Inn, with sixty guests—male, female, and Uncle Chuck—all trying to guess the girth of my midsection, all making the same joke about how I look like I could give birth at any moment. I get it. I'm large. I've gained forty pounds. Remind me to laugh at *their* bodies come Christmas, when I've slimmed down, and they've all been gorging on cheese.

"We have a winner!" Tanya announces at last, dangling a comically long piece of yellow yarn in the air. "Uncle Chuck!"

This is not happening.

Chuck comes bounding up to Tanya as if he's won a cruise

vacation rather than a five-dollar gift card to Dunkin Donuts. I resist the urge to punch him in the stomach.

"I knew it!" he says. "I measured out the yarn, and when I thought she couldn't possibly be that big, I added on an extra coupla inches! Watch out everybody, she might pop!" He laughs like a complete idiot and all the guests start applauding. I slowly count to three in my head.

"No more games," I say, turning to Tanya. "I'm really tired."

"Aw," she says, frowning. "But we still have Pin the Diaper on the—"

"Are we doing gifts now? We should do gifts!" interrupts Babette. She's materialized in front of us, whirling a glass of champagne in the air. She and John flew in last week from Sunset Havens and haven't fully acclimated to the real world yet. They've rented a house and will be staying up north until after the baby's born—news that wasn't met with much joy from Mom and Dad, who had been reveling in the idea of being the only grandparents within driving distance.

"Yes! Let's do gifts!" I say, grateful to get away from Tanya and whatever she was about to pin a diaper on. "Mom! We're doing gifts!"

Poor Mom. I know that planning this shower must have been more than she could handle, but she never let on. And now that Babette's in town, she's been trying even harder to appear calm, cool, and collected. They both follow me toward the back of the room where the gifts are piled on the floor. The bags are mostly in pastel shades of yellow and green, since we aren't finding out if we're having a boy or a girl until delivery day. It's driving Mom and Dad absolutely bonkers, which just adds to the fun.

"She should sit," says Babette, pulling over a folding chair.

"Of course she should!" says Mom, pulling over the padded chair that she decorated with streamers and balloons.

"Oh," says Babette. "That's lovely. Somebody should get this on video!"

"Obviously," says Mom. She snaps her fingers and the videographer comes over. "Set up the tripod, Jason. We're about to begin."

"Wow," says Babette, somewhat taken aback. "Okay. How about a drink, then? Maybe a nice virgin Piña Colada?"

"Oy!" says Mom.

"What?"

"You can't trust these hotel bartenders," says Mom. "They'll fill it with alcohol. What do they care? How about a water?"

"Um, yeah," I say. "Water would be great. Thanks."

Mom smiles triumphantly and hurries off toward the bar. Graham plops into the empty seat beside me. "I'll take that Piña Colada, Mom. Full strength." Babette scurries after Mom, happy to still be needed.

"You're a good son," I say.

Graham laughs. "Joan's really taking care of business today, huh? I'm impressed."

"She is," I say. "I'm proud of her. I hope your mom isn't too offended."

"My mother had the wedding. She'll get over it."

"Good," I say, picking a random gift bag up off the floor. Inside, I glimpse the breast pump that we ended up registering for, just in case. I quickly put the bag down and kick it under the chair with my heel. "Hand me another one, would you?"

Graham hands me another bag with a card sticking out of the top. *We thought you might need this! With love, Janice, Francine, and Roger.* Inside the gift bag is a book. *Sex After Childbirth.* Honestly.

"It was sweet of them to send this along," I say to Babette, quickly shoving the book back into the bag. "How are those three doing?"

"Alive and well!" says Babette.

"That's nice," I say. "Especially after everyone thinking they were dead."

"They certainly left us hanging after the wedding," agrees Babette. "Then, twenty-four hours later, they turn up for half-priced appetizers at Red Lobster!" She shrugs.

We've been opening gifts for about twenty minutes when I begin to tire of everybody's eyes on me, gauging my reaction to each item. I mean, I'm thankful for all the gifts. It's just, how excited can one look after opening their third package of Diaper Genie refills? I'm considering asking for a bathroom break when a voice comes over the intercom.

"Excuse me, folks. But I've been asked to announce that we will be offering open bar for the next hour. Open bar for the next hour." As the intercom clicks off, masses of guests begin rising from their chairs, heading toward the bar like moths to a flame. All interest in me gone.

"Did you do this?" I whisper ecstatically to Graham.

"I told the bartender to give you a twenty-minute head start. I figured by then everyone would be bored, and you'd be ready for a break."

I lean over and give him a kiss on the cheek. "You're the best. How come nobody else has had your baby yet? Wait, don't answer that."

The rest of the gift opening is much more relaxed and enjoyable—at least until Uncle Chuck returns to his table, spills his drink, and loudly announces that his water broke. By the time we get to the last gift, everyone in the room is pretty well sauced, and I'm completely exhausted. I rip the paper off a huge box to find the car seat and stroller system from our registry. Mom and Dad already told us that they were getting it, and they're super excited and proud to finally show it off. As Graham and I are posing next to the box for photos, I see John come through the door at the front of the room. He's slowly winding his way through all the tables...pushing a stroller. It has balloons tied to it, a giant teddy bear strapped into the seat, and looks like it was designed by Elon Musk. Babette jumps up from her seat and takes it from him. She wheels it in front of Mom and Dad's box, and pulls a long, golden lever up the side, clicking it into place. I think this thing has an emergency brake.

"This is *so* embarrassing," she says to Mom. "We had no idea you were buying them a stroller."

Mom looks totally deflated.

"It's fine," I say. "We can use two strollers! Or, we can send one back." Seeing as how Babette and John's stroller is fully assembled, without any tags, and looks as if it were shipped in from SpaceX headquarters, it's pretty obvious which one would end up getting sent back. "Or, Mom and Dad can keep this one at their house," I add, quickly, patting the box. "We can *definitely* use two strollers. It's no biggie at all."

I smile at Mom. She smiles back. Barely.

Damn it.

∽

"Where did they even *get* this thing?" I ask, circling the stroller, which is now parked in the middle of our living room. All the gifts are parked in the middle of our living room. After coming home from the shower yesterday, I went straight to bed without giving any of them a second glance. Today, Mom and Babette are coming over to help me sort them all out. Their idea, not mine.

Graham is sitting on the couch, flipping through the instruction manual. "This says that it can fold into the size of a briefcase." He puts down the manual and looks at me, totally baffled. "*How?*"

"There's this Stephen King novel about a Buick that's actually a portal to another dimension," I say, gently kicking its oversized tires with my toe. "It just appeared one day. The next thing they knew—" I grasp the handles and give it a rough shake. An air bag explodes out of the snack tray. My screams are muffled by the ear-piercing alarm coming from the control panel.

"What is it doing?!" I yell, as the alarm increases in volume. "Make it stop!"

Graham hurries over and we both start hitting random buttons on the control panel. A nozzle pops out from the side.

"It's going to shoot!" I yell. I step behind Graham, just as a forceful stream of water comes shooting out of the nozzle, soaking the living room carpet. Graham hits more buttons. The stroller starts raising itself up and down on hydraulics, sending the stream of water into the living room window. It ricochets back at us, and I run for cover behind the couch. Graham keeps hitting buttons. Finally, the alarm stops, the water dwindles down to a trickle, and with a loud whoosh of air, the stroller returns to its normal height. The silence is deafening.

"What just happened?" asks Graham. His pants are completely soaked.

"I think you peed yourself," I say, laughing as I heave myself up off the floor. "Is it safe to approach?"

"You must've hit the *cooling mist* button," he says, jabbing his finger at the control panel.

"That was not a *mist*." I push his finger out of the way. "You hit *this* one. I saw you. See the flames? This stroller is equipped to put out fires."

Graham just stares at the button. "But, *why*? Who would manufacture such a thing?" He looks at me, speechless. I don't think I've ever seen Graham quite so flummoxed. We both start laughing.

"I bet it's got a flux capacitor in there," I say. "Maybe if we get it up to eighty-eight miles per hour we can send it back to the future."

"Speaking of sci-fi," says Graham, as the doorbell rings. "Our mothers have arrived. I'll be upstairs. Asleep."

I give him a threatening look as I head to the front door. I can already hear Mom and Babette bickering on the doorstep. I watch them through the peephole for a few seconds. Mom is giving her opinion on our house having a stream in the backyard. Babette thinks it'll be nice for the baby to be able to watch the wildlife. Mom says something about deer ticks and Lyme disease. I open the door.

"Hello, hello!" says Babette, kissing me on both cheeks. "We were just talking about how lovely your house is. So woodsy!"

"Thanks," I say, looking at Mom over Babette's shoulder. "We've started leaving food in the backyard so the animals will be comfortable coming closer to the house."

"Oy!" Mom staggers into the coatrack.

"I'm kidding. Come on in." I lead them into the now soggy living room. Water droplets are running down the bay window. "I would stay away from the stroller, though."

"What happened?" asks Babette, looking concerned. "You like it, don't you? It cost a *fortune*."

"I can tell," I say, gingerly attempting to shove the deflated air bag back into its compartment. I'm still not convinced an otherworldly being isn't going to emerge from the storage basket. "It's just going to take some getting used to. Where exactly did you get it?"

"One of John's golf buddies invested in this company out of Japan. *Very* high tech, top-of-the-line stuff. Everyone is using them over there. When the three of you fly down to visit, it folds into the size of a magazine and slides right under the seat!"

Somehow I doubt that thing would make it through security.

Mom rolls her eyes, still sore about being upstaged. Or, up-gifted.

"It's great, Babette," I say. "It's just...it might be too much. We really didn't need you and John to spend so much money."

"Please!" She bats a hand at me. "This is our first grandchild! And since we're not going to be around as much as Richard and Joan, it was the least we could do."

Mom perks up a bit. "When will you be going back to Florida?"

"September," says Babette.

"Ah," says Mom, smiling. "Well before the baby says its first words."

"*Mom.*" I can read her mind. She's worried the baby will call Babette "Grandma" before her.

"Don't worry," says Mom. "I'll send you some pictures. Richard and I will be babysitting. *Daily.*"

Before Babette can respond, Mom pulls a pair of scissors from her purse and starts snipping tags off all the baby clothes—including the ones I was considering exchanging. She tosses each item into a laundry basket.

"I'll have all of these washed for you by tomorrow," she says. "And when we babysit, I will continue to do the baby's laundry." She says this in a very robotic, matter-of-fact tone. Poor Babette.

"Why don't we go see the nursery?" I ask. "Babette, you haven't even seen it yet! I'd love your opinion on the color scheme."

"Color scheme," says Mom, rolling her eyes. "It's *gray*. The baby's going to be colorblind just because its parents didn't want to find out if they were having a boy or a girl."

"That's not how it works, Mom," I say. "Besides, once we find out, we're going to add some pops of color."

I lead them upstairs and into the nursery. I did go on a bit of a splurge in the Pottery Barn catalog. It's true that everything is light gray and white, but it's going to look gorgeous whether we end up adding bits of blue or bits of pink. I feel so calm whenever I come in here. Although, Graham's had a hard time coming to terms with the lack of color. He was really into this crib bedding set called *Havana Nights* that I had to put the kibosh on.

"Oy!" shrieks Mom.

"What?"

"You can't hang those there!" She's pointing at the row of gray wooden elephants hanging on the wall behind the crib. "They'll fall on the baby!"

"We don't exactly get earthquakes around here," I say. "They're not going to fall."

"Who hung them?"

"Graham."

"Oh," says Mom, relaxing. "Okay, then."

Mom doesn't trust me to hang anything on a wall. Graham, on the other hand, could lay a sword across two thumbtacks and she'd happily stand beneath it.

Babette walks over to the changing table and picks up a diaper. "Oh, look at this tiny thing." She holds it up to her cheek. "Can you even remember them being this small, Joan?" She looks at Mom, who joins her at the changing table and picks up another diaper.

"It's hard," she says, turning the diaper over in her hands. "But I do remember some things. Like how carefully we drove home from the hospital when Eric was born."

"I remember that, too," says Babette, sighing and taking a seat in the glider. "And I remember the *fear* we had when we left that hospital. We couldn't believe that they were just letting us take Graham home. That he was *ours*."

"I know," says Mom. "It was terrifying that they trusted us."

Babette laughs. "It's going to be interesting being the grandparents this time around, don't you think? We'll get to spoil them and send them home to their parents. We never have to be the bad guys."

"Well," says Mom, glancing nervously at me. "We're going to be the *full-time* babysitters. We're going to have to have *some* rules."

"Oh, please," says Babette. "You're going to spoil that baby rotten and you know it."

Mom's face breaks into a smile. "Of course we are!" she whispers.

Mom and Babette both laugh and start talking about the ridiculous things that *their* parents used to do when Eric, Graham, and I were babies. Without a word, I slowly back out of the room, partially closing the door behind me.

"You know," I hear Babette say. "John and I are so glad that the baby's going to have you and Richard close by."

"Oh?" says Mom.

"I suppose that's the reason we bought that ridiculous stroller," says Babette. "We feel some guilt over not being around. It was easy to move to Florida once Graham became an adult. But now, with a new baby..." Babette sighs. "It's going to be harder."

"You're not...thinking of moving back, are you?" asks Mom.

"Oh, no," says Babette. I can practically feel Mom's relief oozing through the crack in the door. "It's too late for that. Florida is our home now. But I'm going to need you, Joan, to keep me in the loop. Graham's not going to tell me anything useful when I call. I need *you* to keep me up to date with videos and pictures. Do you know how to FaceTime? I was hoping we could FaceTime during the day, while the kids are at work."

"Of course," says Mom. "That would be lovely."

Note to self: Teach Mom how to FaceTime.

"Good," says Babette. "I feel much better now. And I'm sorry about the stroller situation. I should have checked with you first. I actually received an email this morning that it's been recalled, but I didn't want to disappoint the kids just yet. Anyway, have I ever told you about the time John's mother, the meddling old bat, had the nerve to—"

I slowly back away from the door, and bump into Graham.

"How's it going?" he asks.

I hold a finger over my lips and nod my head toward the nursery. "Aren't they cute?" I whisper.

Graham peeks through the crack. "Let's go watch Netflix," he whispers. "Before they get bored."

"Good idea."

"Did you turn on the baby monitor?"

"Of course." I hold up the receiver that I nicked before leaving the room. I flick it on, getting an earful of dirt about Graham's meddling grandmother, and we quietly creep back down the stairs.

NINE MONTHS

5

I heard that women are three times more likely to DIE from a C-section than a vaginal because of blood clots and infections. Why take that risk????

It was so CLINICAL. There was this big curtain thingy and so much tugging and pulling. I didn't feel INVOLVED. Don't u want to be INVOLVED in your baby's birth????

I heard the pain is excruciating! Stitches and staples...NO THANKS!! I'm going natural and I think ALL women should stop being selfish and do WHATEVER they can to go natural.

I stare miserably at the computer screen.

I'm back on the mommy boards. Not that I ever went off the mommy boards; I just wised up and stopped telling Graham about all the horror stories I've been reading. The trouble is, without Graham's talent for filtering the truth out of the hysterical exaggerations, the horror stories have been left to swirl around in my head, completely unchecked. Today, I'm researching the pros and cons of C-sections. As of right now, I'm planning on a natural birth with loads of painkillers. But there's always the chance that I'll need to have a C-section. I must admit, the thought of not having to push a Thanksgiving turkey out of my body wasn't sounding like the worst thing in the world. Prior to getting on the mommy boards, I kind of had my fingers crossed that I would need one. Now, I feel like a total selfish failure if I don't do everything possible to avoid one.

Why must I always feel so different? All the other moms-to-be are salivating over the prospect of a natural birth. They're casually tossing the word *vaginal* around like it's a pack of M&M's. They can't wait to find out how far Mother Nature will allow certain parts of their bodies to stretch. Meanwhile, I'm terrified. I don't want to find that information out. Ever. There is zero part of me that is looking forward to the birthing process. I don't *care* if there's a curtain, and it's clinical, and Bob Vila has to fasten me back together with a staple gun. I just want to get to the part where the baby is outside of my body, and we get to feed it and dress it in onesies. I mean, if I adopted a baby I wouldn't have to go through the pain of childbirth. Why must I be so judged for wanting to avoid it?

I'm about to go find Graham and admit to what I've been reading, when a sudden pain in my abdomen stops me in my tracks. It's a sharp, gassy sort of a pain. I sit back down. A few minutes later, I feel it again. I take out my phone and turn on the stopwatch. Exactly seven minutes apart. Crap. I'm not due for another week. I was supposed to have another week to stress myself out and obsess over everything I'm doing wrong.

I'm not ready.

"Graham!" I shout into the depths of the house. "GRAHAM!!"

Graham comes bounding down the stairs, five at a time. "What? What's wrong?"

"I'm having contractions."

"Braxton Hicks?"

"No, real ones."

"Are you sure?"

"I think so. They're like these stabby, gassy sort of pains."

"Oh. Well, maybe you just need to—"

"They're seven minutes apart."

"Oh."

"Yeah. *Oh.*"

Graham just looks at me, wide-eyed, then runs back up the stairs, five at a time. When he comes back down, he's carrying The Duffle.

"Where have you been hiding *that*?" I ask.

"Hall closet. This thing holds way more than that suitcase you packed. It's incredible."

"We're not carrying that thing into the hospital! What's even in there? Mom and Dad's underwear? *Mom and Dad*?"

Graham laughs. "Just our clothes, some snacks, and this guy —" He pulls out the giant teddy bear that came with John and Babette's stroller.

"Graham, the baby's eyes are going to be all gooped shut. He's not even going to be able to see that! Also, I'm pretty sure it's a suffocation hazard."

"It's to brighten up the room, Sum. It's not going in the crib. I just don't want it to be all cold and clinical at the hospital."

At the words *cold and clinical,* I remember the reason I was about to go and look for Graham. I step closer and clutch his arm. "I can't do this," I say.

"I didn't expect you to," he says. "I'll carry The Duffle."

"Not *that*. This—" I motion to my stomach. The elephant in the room. "I can't have this baby. There's no good way of getting it out. I've done all the research, Graham, and it's bad news. It's infections, and blood clots and, God help me, episiotomies! We should have thought about all this before!"

Now I'm really starting to panic. I'm not an idiot. This baby is coming out whether I like it or not. The process has already begun and there's nothing I can do to stop it. I'm on a runaway train that's not stopping until I've been sufficiently tortured, beaten, and maimed. I get a vivid picture in my mind of Linda in the delivery room. She's totally drug-free and smiling in ecstasy. Babies are floating effortlessly out from between her legs. I want to strangle her. Instead, tears start streaming down my cheeks.

Graham pries my stiff fingers out of his arm and grips me firmly by the shoulders. "Look at me."

I stare stubbornly down at the carpet.

"Look at me," he says again, bending down and getting right in my face. I look up.

"Your mother had two children, Summer. *Your mother.* Joan Hartwell went into labor twice, and she was *fine.* Okay? The same woman who couldn't make it through a hot stone massage, gave birth *twice.* I know you're scared, and I know that I have no idea what you're going through, but what I do know is that if *she* survived childbirth, so will you."

I let out a choking, snorty sort of a laugh, and wipe away some tears.

"You're going to be okay," he says. "I promise. And I'm going to be there with you the whole time."

He does succeed in making me feel slightly better, but the nagging awareness that I will ultimately be going through this alone—no matter who's standing next to me, holding my hand—sends a fresh set of tears pouring down my cheeks. Then another contraction begins. I take a seat on the couch while Graham starts the stopwatch. I close my eyes. What started out as a minor gas pain is really starting to suck.

Five minutes apart.

"Time to go," he says, helping me up and kissing me on the forehead. "We've got to get to the hospital. We're going to have a baby!" The expression on his face is seventy percent calm, reassuring husband, and thirty percent insane person about to leap through a plate glass window. He pulls me in for a hug. We stand there for a moment, savoring the quiet. It's bittersweet, knowing this is the last time it will be just the two of us living in this house. But it's also exciting. We're bringing a whole new life into the world! Someone who's going to develop a totally original set of childhood memories. Someone who's going to have Joan and Richard Hartwell for grandparents, and an Uncle Eric, and a Great Uncle Chuck. Someone whose dad invented an iPhone app that farts. Someone who's going to spend a good portion of their summer vacations at a place called Sunset Havens.

Note to self: Apologize to baby.

The tears continue for the entire drive to the hospital, partly due to road construction causing us to bump along like we've taken a horse and buggy.

"Why didn't we plan for this?" I moan. "Why didn't we look for a different route?"

"I don't know," says Graham, looking seriously panicked. "I'm sorry! I just didn't think of it! How are you doing?"

I try to concentrate on my breathing as we thump over a series of steel plates.

"Fine," I say, gritting my teeth.

"We're almost there." He reaches over to squeeze my hand as masses of loose gravel fly around beneath the car.

"You should call our parents!" I yell over the din. It sounds like we're being shot at. It would actually be a hilarious time to call Mom, if I were in a better frame of mind.

"I will!" yells Graham. "Once you're settled in a room!"

A police officer waves us through an obstacle course of traffic cones and raised manhole covers, until finally we see the sign for the hospital.

Graham turns wildly into the driveway and comes to a screeching halt in front of the main entrance which, I'm sure, was totally good for the baby. He jumps out of the car, helps me into a wheelchair, then heaves The Duffle out of the trunk. As I watch, I have a brief, pleasant memory of him swinging The Duffle onto the roof of his Camaro, some years ago. Another painful contraction quickly puts a damper on it. If it weren't for that cruise, I wouldn't be in this situation right now. I could be in my parents' basement, watching *Doctor Who*. Skinny. Single. Pain free. I suddenly understand all those movies where the pregnant wife is screaming belligerently at her husband, "Why did you do this to me?!"

I watch the valet drive off with the family-friendly, four-door sedan that's replaced Graham's yellow Camaro. Actually, a red Jaguar F-type has replaced Graham's yellow Camaro. But it's home at the moment.

It's strange to think that the next time we get inside our car, there'll be three of us. Again, I picture Graham swinging The Duffle onto the roof of his car and fastening it into place with bungee cords. I picture the two of us in the front seat, music blasting, Mom and Dad in the back. I was all nerves and attitude that day, with an idiotic plan to find a husband. I could never have fathomed that this is where we would end up. I would never have guessed that I would someday be bringing the next generation of Blenderman DNA into the world. A scary thought, on so many levels.

I smile up at Graham as he swivels the wheelchair around, and we go inside the hospital.

∽

THE MOMMY BOARDS WERE RIGHT.

The top half of me is hidden back here behind this mint green curtain, while the lower half of me is getting tugged and yanked, like it's being put through some sort of Looney Tunes contraption. Like Bugs Bunny is operating the levers, and the lower half of me is going to come out wearing a tutu and lipstick.

Only, it's not funny like that. It's clinical, and scary, and beyond bizarre. Although the nurses are all very sweet. They keep coming over to reassure me that everything is going well and checking to see if I need anything. I don't exactly feel like the "victim of an alien probing," as one Internet mom so eloquently put it. Graham, as promised, is sitting right next to me, up here by my head. He's bravely peeked around the curtain a few times—hopefully not witnessing my uterus flopped out on the table or anything—and then reported back looking, to be honest, completely wretched.

I can't blame him. This whole thing has been nerve-wracking. The nurses spent nearly an hour asking me to push—with no progress being made—before the baby's heart rate began to drop. That's when they told Graham to change into scrubs, and they whooshed me off to the operating room for an emergency C-section. Now, I can't feel a thing, but I'm being yanked and tugged, and the doctors keep saying gory things that make me want to vomit, and the waiting is just killing us.

Until finally, like a ray of sunshine slicing through all the scary stuff, comes the sound of crying. Graham and I look at each other, full of hope. Tears are streaming down both of our faces. *Finally*. I was getting tired of sobbing alone.

"It's a girl!" announces one of the doctors.

A girl!

I have a daughter. Graham has a daughter. That might just be the sweetest thought I've ever had. A moment later, a tiny morsel wrapped in a pink and white hospital blanket is held down for me to see. Her little face is all cheeks and tiny, pink jelly-bean lips. Her eyes are shut tightly against the bright overhead lights. A few moments ago, all she knew was peace, and quiet, and floating. And then suddenly it was chaos, bright lights, and cold. *I'm so sorry,* I think. *It'll be better soon. I promise.* With that thought comes the realization that I'm going to spend the rest of my life trying to make her life better.

"Hello, Sarah Michelle," I whisper.

Here's the thing. I watched a *lot* of *Buffy the Vampire Slayer* during the last few weeks of my pregnancy, and I have no living relatives named either Sarah or Michelle. Plus, it's a lovely name. Even Mom seemed to like it. Of course, I didn't mention the namesake-being-a-vampire-slayer bit. What Mom doesn't know about pop culture won't hurt her.

Much too quickly, Sarah is whisked away again to be measured and weighed. Graham goes with her and I lay my head back down to rest. The doctors are finishing up on the other side of the curtain.

"You can go ahead and put the uterus back in," says one of them, to a med student. I *knew* it. No wonder Graham looked so pale. Remind me to never again give birth at a teaching hospital. It's like OBGYN 101 down there. Speaking of which, why is the med student putting me back together? Shouldn't they be practicing on a dummy, or an orange, or a kid who fell off his bike? I just had major surgery here. If they forget a scalpel inside of me, they're dead meat.

Or, I suppose, I'll be dead meat.

On that cheerful note, I'm lifted from the operating table to a gurney, and wheeled back to my room to rest. I'm loving the fact that I don't need to pee. I know there's nothing glamorous about a urinary catheter; but there sure is something magnificent about knowing I won't have to get up and walk to the bathroom any time soon.

A short time later, Graham appears in the room, followed by a nurse pushing Sarah in a bassinet. She hands her to me carefully, wrapped in a blanket—all weighed, measured, and approved—finally ours to hold. Ours to *keep*. Now I know what

Babette was talking about. How do the nurses and doctors know that we can be trusted? How do they know that we're not going to be the worst parents in the world?

Graham squeezes onto the bed next to me, and suddenly the three of us have formed the classic mom/dad/baby arrangement that has invaded my Facebook feed so many times over the past year. That one photograph that caused me such bitterness and jealousy when we were trying unsuccessfully to conceive, month after month. Yet, here we are. Our turn at last.

"We need someone to take the picture!" I say, starting to panic. Not *a* picture, but *the* picture. The picture that will pop up in my Facebook Memories, year after year, on Sarah's birthday. The one that I'll someday share with the caption, *Remember when she was this small??* I'm about to ask the nurse to take a picture with Graham's phone, when there's a sudden commotion in the hall.

"Congratulations!!"

Babette is first through the door, singing congratulations in her high-pitched, singsong voice. She's followed by John, carrying a bunch of pink and blue balloons. Behind John are Mom and Dad, carrying an enormous Edible Arrangement, followed by Eric and Tanya, excitedly bringing up the rear. They've got about six hundred cameras between them. Once the family photo is taken, I relax a bit. At least until Mom, Babette, and Tanya pull away from the pack, zero in on the baby, and seem to float toward me, toes dragging on the ground, like a scene from *The Craft*. I shrink back, pulling Sarah in closer to my chest.

Back, you devils!

"She's absolutely beautiful," whispers Babette.

"Oy," breathes Mom. "She's a doll!"

"My niece," murmurs Tanya.

Graham's been completely squeezed out of the scene, reappearing at the foot of the bed where he shakes hands with John, Dad, and Eric. Eric's pulled out a box of cigars and a flask, earning a reproachful look from the nurse. It's nice, though, that he's excited. Graham takes a swig from the flask and gives me a wink. If it's going to help him forget everything he saw on the far side of that curtain, by all means, drink away.

"How are you feeling?" asks Mom, snapping her head up, suddenly remembering that I still exist. "I almost fainted when I heard you needed a C-section. You mustn't do any exercise. Or lifting. If you lift something that's too heavy, you'll rip the stitches. Let Graham do everything. And if he's not home, call your father. I'll send him over."

"I'm not going to ask my seventy-year-old father to lift something heavy for me," I say. "And don't worry about exercising. I wasn't planning on going back to the gym until Tuesday."

"Oy! Richard!"

"What?"

"She thinks she's going to the gym on Tuesday!"

Dad's smiling, new-grandfather face is quickly replaced by the look of somebody who's dropped a safe on their foot.

"But she can't!" he cries, waving around the spindly arms that are supposed to do all my heavy lifting.

"I was *kidding*," I say, rolling my eyes. "Of course I'm not going to the gym."

Note to self: Don't tell Mom and Dad when I go to the gym.

Mom lets out a sigh of relief.

"*Anyway*," I continue. "I feel fine. All that worrying about having a C-section, and it was *fine*. I'm just tired. Besides, I've got this—" I hold up the morphine button and give it a couple of enthusiastic clicks.

Dad's face returns to normal, and he's once more beaming at us from the end of the bed. He's too timid to approach the wall of estrogen currently fencing Sarah in, but I'll make sure he has a turn to hold her later on. I'm also glad to see some color has returned to Graham's cheeks. Or, maybe it's just because he's changed out of the drab hospital scrubs and into a bright green T-shirt. Why he ever thought we needed a teddy bear to brighten up the room is beyond me. He's like a traveling ball of sunshine. I smile down at Sarah. Now I have two.

As I look at her face, I wonder what it's going to be like for her, growing up with Graham for a father? Will he plop her onto a Jet Ski and force her to get a tattoo? Will he take her cliff diving in Jamaica and snorkeling with stingrays in Antigua?

The poor child didn't sign up for any of that. *I* did. Now, whether she likes it or not, she's going to be thrust into a life of unpredictable spontaneity. That's when the thought occurs to me that her Blenderman DNA might not only be good for cutting her anxiety level in half, and increasing her skin pigmentation, but, personality-wise, it might make her turn out exactly like her father.

She might *want* to do all those things, and more. She might like motorcycles, and bad boys, and backpacking across Europe. She might want to skydive, and parasail, and climb Mount Everest. Graham might finally get a taste of what it's been like to be *me* these past few years. It's kind of nice to think of us both being on even ground. Both of us anxious and terrified over the well-being of our daughter.

As I mull over these thoughts, and the morphine kicks in, Mom takes the baby out of my arms. The sound of everyone's incessant babbling starts to blend into a dull, comforting roar. I close my eyes and drift off. Real life, and the eternity of overwhelming, parental anxiety that now goes along with it, can begin tomorrow.

For now...sleep.

MATERNITY LEAVE

6

"Sarah?"

The nurse has barely finished calling us in before Dad scoops up the car seat and takes off through the door to the exam rooms. Mom wasn't kidding when she said she didn't want me lifting anything. The other day, she threw an entire shepherd's pie across the room, trying to stop me from picking up a sock. She claims she thought I was trying to lift the ottoman. Dad's been suffering the brunt of it, though, retrieving baskets full of laundry from the basement and carrying grocery bags in from the car. He's developed this superhuman grandpa strength over the past couple of weeks. Which, you know, good for him. But, for me, it's a bit embarrassing. Never mind that his coordination isn't quite what it used to be.

"I said *I* wanted to carry it!" I hiss, scurrying along behind him.

"I've got it!" he says, cheerfully, bumping into a doorframe.

"Dad!"

"What?"

"She's getting all jostled!" I reach over and try to pry the handle out of his hands. "Let *me* carry it!"

"You can't carry that!" shrieks Mom, reaching between us and grabbing the handle. The nurse glances back to find the three of us all trotting along with our hands on the car seat, like some sort of weird family from *The X-Files*. Mom and I are tripping over each other, and Dad's already knocked a box of cotton swabs off one of the counters. The nurse gives us an awkward, *I'm just going to go ahead and call social services* sort of smile, before ushering us quickly into a room.

We're at a doctor's appointment for my newborn child, and I feel more like a little kid than I have in years. It's all this waitress at Applebee's fault. She went and told Mom that she ripped her stitches putting a lasagna pan in the oven, and I've yet to hear the end of it. What I would like to know is why my parents were discussing such things with a waitress at Applebee's? *Baked haddock, please. Rice pilaf. Caesar salad. That reminds me, our daughter had a Caesarean last night. No anchovies. And by what methods have you given birth?*

I wouldn't put it past them.

After a brief barrage of questions from the nurse, we're left alone again in the exam room. I pull a bottle out of the diaper bag and give Sarah a quick feeding before the doctor comes in. Last time, I forgot to bring one and she screamed her head off for half the appointment. The doctor definitely made a note in her permanent file. *Mother incompetent.* Mom definitely made a mental note in her permanent file. *Daughter incompetent.* I'm learning as I go.

"You know," I say, shifting Sarah in my arms. "I would have liked to carry my own child into her appointment. It's been two weeks since my surgery. We looked like a bunch of clowns out there."

"But the waitress at Applebee's—"

"I don't want to hear about the waitress at Applebee's! Sarah is a baby, not a lasagna pan!"

"You're missing the point," says Mom.

"No, *you're* missing the point."

Mom rolls her eyes. "What if Graham were here? Would you let *him* carry the baby?"

"Of course," I say. "He's the father. Plus, Graham's not seventy years old. People must think I'm a spoiled princess, making an old man carry my heavy stuff around. No offense, Dad."

Dad shrugs.

"If we're so embarrassing," says Mom, "why don't you just schedule the next appointment for when Graham is available? Where is he again?"

"He had a meeting in Boston," I say.

Graham and Eric are pitching one of their apps to a tech company today. They're probably playing laser tag on hoverboards, while I'm sitting on a metal exam table arguing with my parents—who, by the way, are standing underneath a rack full of colorful pamphlets titled, "What's Happening to My Body?" I let out a giggle.

"What?" asks Mom.

"Nothing," I say, feeling a bit better. A giggle always puts things into perspective. "Look, it's just hard to feel like a mom, when your parents insist on treating you like a baby."

"I give up," says Mom. "Let's let her carry the heavy stuff, Richard. Let's let her. Then when she rips her stitches and ends up in the hospital, oh well!" She rolls her eyes and throws her hands in the air. *Nothing we could do about it!*

"Why am I never allowed to have my own opinion?" I ask. "Why are my feelings always wrong?" Sarah starts fussing in my arms and I lower my voice. The poor kid can already sense the tension between us. Who am I kidding? She probably sensed it in the womb.

"We're not trying to *baby* you," whispers Dad, in his attempt at mediating the situation. "We just worry. You know how we are. Don't take us too seriously." He's jammed his hands into the pockets of his cargo pants and is nervously jiggling his keys around. I try not to giggle again as he's still standing beneath the "What's Happening to My Body?" sign. Mom's taken a seat and is tapping away at her phone, demonstrating just how completely she's given up on me.

"I know," I say, rolling my eyes. As usual, I'm unable to stay angry with Dad. "I do appreciate you coming with me today. I wasn't trying to be ungrateful."

He walks over and pats me gently on the shoulder, smiling down at the baby. Mom doesn't budge.

The actual appointment is rather uneventful. As soon as the doctor comes in, Mom transforms from Joan Jekyll back into doting grandmother, answering most of the questions for me, and asking if it's safe to take the baby out of the house due to the approach of flu season. It's July, mind you.

It's early afternoon when we return home, and Mom and Dad have no intention of leaving us yet. We picked up sandwiches on the way, and Mom is busy spreading everything out on the kitchen table. Sarah is asleep in her car seat. She'll be hungry again when she wakes up. And she'll need her diaper changed. It's a never-ending cycle. Feedings, diaper changes. Diaper changes, feedings.

I think I have a touch of postpartum depression, if we're being honest. I'm happy that Sarah's here, of course. It's just that as soon as Graham arrives home later in the day, I've taken to sobbing uncontrollably. Like clockwork, Mom and Dad leave, Graham comes home, I start sobbing. Boom, boom, boom. Once I've finished, I turn on *The Golden Girls*, we eat dinner, and everything is cheery again. Hopefully, it passes. I'm still pretty jacked up on pregnancy hormones, so I'm not too concerned. I know that life will get back to normal once Sarah is a little older, and I return to work. But, right now, I can't seem to see past the next few hours.

The next...few...hours.

Let's see. Those shall consist of me and my parents sitting around the living room watching *Days of Our Lives*. Babette will probably come over later, and then we'll all go for a walk. I shudder as I take a seat at the kitchen table.

It's really not that bad. I *know* that. It's been a beautiful summer. I have a healthy child, and I'm surrounded by family that loves me. I'm very, very lucky. It's just that I was so used to being independent. I've always enjoyed being alone. Now, I can't foresee ever being alone again. And I don't mean "alone" in the sense that I don't want to be married anymore, or that I regret having a baby. I just mean that I would love to go for a peaceful walk, alone with Sarah, thinking my own thoughts and walking at my own pace. Instead, I've got a mother and a mother-in-law fiddling with blankets and adjusting sun visors. Constantly advising, and judging, and swatting away invisible insects like they're both on acid trips. It's exhausting.

I think that's why I've been crying every time Graham gets home. It's not out of sadness; it's out of relief. The relief of the day being almost over. The promise of finally being able to recharge, just the two of us, after having my batteries completely drained.

I take a few bites of my ham and cheese. Mom says something about hemming the baby's pants. I'm not really listening. All I can hear is the sound of Dad chewing. Lettuce, pickles, Italian meats, all sloshing around between his teeth. I get up and turn on the television to drown him out.

"LIKE SANDS THROUGH THE HOURGLASS!"

I scramble for the volume button as the *Days of Our Lives* intro comes blaring out of the speakers. Graham and I were watching Netflix last night, and it always screws with the volume. Damn it. Sarah stirs, blinks her eyes, and lets loose with a full-blast, *HOW CAN IT BE THAT NOBODY IS FEEDING ME*, type howl. Great. I should have warmed a bottle for her before I sat down to eat. Why didn't I think of that? Now, she's going to scream for the next five minutes while I stand there running one under warm water, with Mom taking mental notes about my incompetence.

Breathe, Summer.

Dad puts down his sandwich and offers to hold the baby while I warm up a bottle. Instead of feeling grateful, I think, *At least now I don't have to listen to him chew.* Which I feel bad for thinking—yet, at the same time, irrationally jubilant. As I wait for the bottle to warm, Mom and Dad stare at the television. Bo and Hope have broken up again. John Black might actually be dead this time, but probably not. Who cares? I care. I both care and don't care. I feel simultaneously like a hopeful young mother, and someone who's woken up to inexplicably find herself old—all the excitement and promise of life over. I watch *Days of Our Lives* with my parents now. Yesterday, I watched Dad waterproof his boots.

How much longer until Graham gets home? The clock on the microwave reads 1:06 p.m. The minutes creep along, like sands through the hourglass.

∼

I CAN'T BELIEVE how time has flown. I go back to work on Monday.

Monday!

Two more days and I'm supposed to hand Sarah over to Mom and Dad, jump in my car, and drive away like some sort of free-spirited person with no responsibilities. Two months ago I was freaking out from sitting around watching *Days of Our Lives* and listening to Dad chew. Now, I'm freaking out because it's all going to end. Not so much the soap operas and the loud chewing, but the oodles of quality time I've been spending with Sarah. The leisurely walks, the trips to the mall, even the memories of past diaper changes have been making me nostalgic. Of course, the diaper changes will still be waiting for me the second I walk through the door. But not all the other stuff. The nice stuff.

The idea of becoming a stay at home mom is tempting, though I'll never admit it to Mom. On the other hand, I do miss my work life and adult conversations, even if they're with Linda and on the subject of placenta capsules. It'll be fine. I'll adjust to work just like I ended up adjusting to maternity leave. It took three and a half weeks, but I finally stopped sobbing at the sight of Graham.

"Oh geez," I say, tears starting to trickle down my cheeks.

"Uh-oh," says Graham. "I thought we were past this?"

"We are," I say, wiping them away. "These are good tears. You two are just so adorable."

He's wearing this very Farmer Graham-looking flannel shirt, and carrying Sarah in the Baby Bjorn. We're spending the afternoon apple picking before sending John and Babette back to Florida tomorrow. My idea. It's autumn in New England, so the place is rife with apple picking. And when I say "the place," I mean Facebook. My Facebook feed has been rife with photos of everybody and their uncle—sometimes literally with their uncle—euphorically picking apples. Rachel posted her photos last weekend. Her daughter, who is only four months older than Sarah, was all decked out in a cable-knit sweater, handmade hat, and tiny baby Ugg boots. There were photos of the baby asleep on the grass surrounded by apples. Photos of the baby propped up against a tree surrounded by apples. A photo of the three of them at sunset, silhouetted between two apple trees. Sunset!

The orchard closes at four o'clock. I swear they Photoshopped the entire thing.

All the same, here we are, standing in the parking lot of Brooksby Farm, waiting for Eric and Tanya to arrive. Mom keeps trying to slather sunscreen on Sarah's head, and Babette keeps making wistful comments about what a pity it is that they have to leave tomorrow. I know that she's going to miss the baby, but I also know that she's been itching to get out of here ever since the temperature dropped below seventy-five.

"Here they come," says Graham, as the Escalade pulls into the lot. The farm isn't even open yet, but the parking lot is already filling up. As they pull into a space three aisles over, I start maneuvering the stroller across the grass and rocks. How come nobody posts pictures of this part? I didn't see any photos of Rachel attempting to dislodge her stroller from a set of muddy tire tracks. Thanks a lot, Facebook.

Eric and Tanya jump out of the car, looking oddly excited. Tanya is practically glowing.

"We have an announcement to make!" she says, clasping her hands together.

Oh my God. She *is* glowing. She can't be—

I look over at Mom, who's pressed a hand across her mouth. Yes, she's thinking it too. I knew it! Tanya steps back and flings open the back door of the Escalade.

"We got dogs!"

Two Jack Russells come bounding out, headed straight for Mom. They're going berserk, jumping straight up and down, and barking like mad. Mom screams as the smaller of the two leaps at least six inches above her head. Graham takes a few steps back, wrapping his arms protectively around the Bjorn.

"Aren't they great?" asks Eric, nonchalantly walking over with two leashes. "Sit, fellas!" They ignore him. One squats in front of a tree stump.

"Oh, that's lovely," I say.

"Did we bring the scooper?" asks Eric.

Still looking delighted, Tanya swoops back into the car and returns with a plastic bag and a shovel.

"The thing is, they don't actually allow dogs here," says Eric, as he scoops. "So, we're going to leave. We picked the dogs up this morning and thought we'd stop by to surprise you. You guys have fun, though." He ties up the bag, steps over to say his good-byes to John and Babette, and then they all pile back into the Escalade.

"We'll see you later in the week!" says Tanya, rolling down the window and blowing me a kiss. With a trail of dust, and the fading sound of barking dogs, they're gone.

"Wow," I say, looking up at Graham. "They got dogs."

"Dogs," says Mom, looking as if she's been trampled. Which she pretty much has.

I smile and put my arm around her shoulder. "Graham and I didn't get dogs. Graham and I got a baby." Mom looks at me approvingly, nodding her head. It feels good to be the favorite.

The remaining six of us walk toward the main entrance.

"Oh, no," I breathe. The line to get in is at least four hundred deep. As we take our place at the back of the line, I pull up the farm's website on my phone. "*Thirty-five dollars* for a half bushel?"

Graham's eyebrows shoot up. "Didn't you look any of this up before?"

"All I could think about was getting photos of Sarah surrounded by apples! I was crazed! What are we even going to do with a half bushel of apples? And why did nobody mention *this line*?"

My anxiety level is on the rise. Not only is there this heinous line, but I see a hay wagon slowly loading people from the entrance and driving them off into the orchard. One hay wagon.

Back and forth. This could take all day. And what was I thinking bringing the stupid stroller? I can't take a stroller on a hay wagon. Did I think that Graham was going to get tired from carrying around a ten-pound baby? Did I think that he was going to collapse with exhaustion, using his last ounce of strength to crawl toward the stroller that his wife so fortuitously brought along? Honestly. I suppose I could bring it back to the car, but it's just so far away.

"You know," says Graham, pointing past the crowds. "There's a farm stand over there. We could just buy a bag of apples and take a few photos when we get home. No one will even know the difference. We can grab a pumpkin too. Really give Anne Geddes a run for her money."

I look from Graham, to the farm stand, to the adjoining snack shack with the huge sign for apple cider donuts. I look at each of our parents. Mom still seems stunned about the dogs. Dad's staring uneasily at the hay wagon, jiggling his keys up and down in his pocket. Babette's dodging the swarm of bees that have decided to start harassing us. John has this faraway look in his eyes, already back on the golf course at Sunset Havens.

Okay, screw it.

"Who wants coffee and donuts?" I ask.

Everybody raises their hand. Dad lets out an actual whoop of relief.

We're the only customers in the snack shack. With everybody else foolish enough to be outside picking apples, this was the perfect time to come. The donuts are fresh out of the oven, the coffee piping hot. Graham orders six coffees and a dozen donuts, and we all settle in around a rustic wooden table. Sarah is sound asleep in the stroller. I knew there was a reason I brought it.

"These donuts are out of this world," says Mom, sprinkling cinnamon sugar all over the table.

"We should do this again next year," I say.

"It is nice to indulge once in a while," says Babette, reaching for her second donut. "Back on the diet tomorrow!"

"Oy, please," says Mom. "What do you need to diet for? You're so slim. You could be a model!"

"A Model T," says John, and we all laugh. Babette gently swats him on the arm.

"So, when will you be back to visit?" asks Mom.

"Thanksgiving," says John, with a sigh. "And staying through Christmas."

"Sarah's going to be so much bigger by then," says Babette with a frown.

"It's only two months," I say. "And Mom's going to keep you posted with pictures and videos, right?"

Mom nods. "Eric's teaching me how to skip."

That's an odd visual. Oh, wait. "It's called *Skype*, Mom." I laugh. Mom waves her hand at me, dismissively.

"Well, I'm so glad to hear that," says Babette. "We're going to miss her so much."

"But after Christmas, we're gone until June!" chimes in John, brightening up quite a bit. Babette looks at him and slowly shakes her head.

"Oh, look," says Mom, pointing at the stroller. "She's awake!"

"Nyuck, nyuck, nyuck!" Dad does his best Three Stooges impersonation, and tickles Sarah under the chin. She smiles.

"Why don't you give her to me," says Mom. "I think she wants her grandma."

"Oh, I don't know," says Babette. "I think she wants to come to Grammy."

Both grandmothers make goofy kissy faces, their arms outstretched, as Graham lifts Sarah out of the stroller. I have no idea who he's going to hand her to. If this were a movie, the camera would slowly start to pull away as some sort of cheerful song played in the background, the family still bickering amicably. The happily ever after implied.

In real life, I sit back and sip my coffee. John turns to Dad and mentions that self-driving golf carts might soon be coming to Sunset Havens. Dad jokes that if he got into a self-driving golf cart, it might self-drive itself right into a lake. Graham, in a Judgment of Solomon moment, dangles Sarah between the two grandmothers. Mom claims the head end, and Babette latches onto the feet. A text message comes in from Tanya. They've stopped at a farm stand and taken a series of photos of the dogs, surrounded by apples. I laugh out loud and hold the picture up for Graham to see. "Three Little Birds" starts playing on the radio, and he gives me a wink.

Happily ever after implied.

The End

OTHER BOOKS BY BETH LABONTE

Summer at Sea

Summer at Sunset

Down, Then Up: A Novella

Love Notes in Reindeer Falls

Pumpkin Everything

You can also find Beth on:

Facebook

Twitter

www.bethlabonte.com

TURN THE PAGE FOR A PEEK AT PUMPKIN EVERYTHING

1

"Grandpa's driven through Dunkin' Donuts!"

"So what?" I asked, crinkling my forehead as I walked to the refrigerator. My mother's hysterical tone wasn't quite matching up with the mundane words she spoke into the phone. Leave it to my mother to be overly dramatic about Grandpa going out for a coffee. If anyone had cause to be hysterical and dramatic, it was me. Cheating scumbag fiancé. Wedding canceled. Writing career hanging by a thread thanks to mega case of writer's block, thanks to cheating scumbag fiancé. It had been quite the chain reaction. But had she asked me about any of these tragedies recently? Nope. Here she was freaking out because Grandpa had utilized a drive-through window. I opened the fridge and pulled out a bottle of water. "Drive-throughs are a modern-day convenience, Mom. You might want to try one sometime."

"You're not getting it. He drove *through* a Dunkin' Donuts."

I froze midway through unscrewing the cap. "You don't mean...literally?"

"Yes, *literally*," said Mom. "Your grandfather has literally driven his Jeep through the front window of Dunkin' Donuts! It's probably all over the news! I just got a call from the Autumnboro police. I'm due on-air in ten minutes, Amy, and now I'm visibly shaken. Who wants to order cruise-wear from a person who looks visibly shaken?"

I walked back toward the couch with one hand clamped across my mouth. The police were involved? This was serious. "Is he okay?" I asked, sinking down into the cushions. "Was anyone hurt?" A vision of Grandpa, alone and scared in a courtroom, on trial for involuntary manslaughter, flashed through my mind. He didn't deserve to spend his last remaining years in prison.

"He's fractured his wrist," said Mom. "But nobody else was hurt. Thank God. He claims he was pressing the brake when the car just shot forward! Same old story they all use at that age when they forget which pedal is the accelerator." I could almost hear the eye roll in her voice. "I *knew* this would happen. I knew if I let him keep his driver's license that it was only a matter of time before disaster struck. I never should have left him alone up there."

"He's been up there alone for ten years, Mom. And he's been totally fine until just now." I slumped back into the couch, still processing my relief that Grandpa hadn't killed anybody. "Besides, he loves Autumnboro. You know it would crush him if you made him move."

Autumnboro, New Hampshire—the self-proclaimed Autumn Capital of the World—was bursting with pumpkins, mind-blowing fall foliage, and a population of just over five thousand. It was also the hometown I'd been successfully avoiding since escaping to Penn State ten years ago. A memory of soft green eyes, filled with the sort of sadness I couldn't even begin to understand, invaded my mind, followed by a familiar twang of guilt.

"It's inevitable, Amy," she said. "He's not getting any younger, and we can't keep dealing with these types of things if we're seven hours away. Plus, he didn't kill anybody this time, but next time..."

"Well, I doubt he's going to be driving again anytime soon."

"That's for sure. His Jeep was totaled, and I'm taking away his keys once and for all. For everybody's safety."

I frowned at the definitive tone in her voice...and at the trace of glee. Taking away his keys would eliminate a great deal of her Grandpa-induced stress, of which she'd been having quite a lot lately. Even with five hundred miles between us, our living arrangement with Grandpa had been running fairly smoothly. That was, until six months ago when he'd started calling Mom at all hours—confused about whether or not he'd taken his medication or panicked because he couldn't find his wallet. They were small things, but they'd put the idea in her head that he was getting too old to be living on his own, and now...Dunkin' Donuts.

I wanted him to be safe, of course. But, I also wasn't sure how he would survive on his own in New Hampshire without any wheels. I pictured him alone in his house, surrounded by empty pizza boxes and dead houseplants. Both his landline and his cell phone were dead for some reason, the lights flickering as a grandfather clock mournfully bonged each endless, passing hour. The howling of a lone coyote, his only connection with the outside world. I swallowed past the lump in my throat.

"So, are you taking some time off to go up there?" I asked. "He's probably going to need some help until his wrist is healed." My image of Grandpa surrounded by pizza boxes and dead houseplants was replaced by an image of him pathetically trying to unscrew lids from various jars—jelly, mayonnaise, pickle—as each one slipped from his hand and shattered into sharp, deadly shards on the floor. A barefooted Grandpa crunched down on them like Marv from *Home Alone*. I shuddered.

"You know I can't go up there," Mom said, indignantly. "They've got me working nonstop straight through Christmas. I'm with Isaac Mizrahi every night this week, and they're flying Dennis Basso in on Saturday to showcase his new Christmas ornaments. Take time off? Pffft!"

I rolled my eyes as she scoffed loudly into the phone. She was always going on about Isaac Mizrahi. My mother hosted her own show on QVC—that's the home shopping channel headquartered down here in Pennsylvania—called *Sharyn's Closet*. She'd auditioned for the spot as soon as I'd accepted my admissions offer to Penn State, citing it as her secret, lifelong dream. Personally, I think her secret, lifelong dream was to get the heck out of Autumnboro as soon as I'd finished high school. Whatever the case, QVC booked her for the show, and she and Dad followed me south, leaving Grandpa alone up in New Hampshire. I saw a flash of those tragic green eyes again. Not Grandpa's. His were blue and merry and buried beneath two white puffs of eyebrows. The green ones weren't family, but they'd also been left behind—and the reason I'd gone, to be honest.

"So, what then?" I sighed, running my hand over the soft leather couch, suddenly wishing I had a nine-to-five office job, a husband, and kids. Anything to use as an excuse not to go up to Autumnboro myself. But I wrote horror novels from home—after college I'd become a bit of a self-published success story—and my cheating scumbag fiancé had moved out two months ago. Writer's block had settled in as soon as the wedding was canceled, meaning my days and nights were now filled by staring wide-eyed at stark white Word documents. I was alone, devoid of responsibilities, and at risk of developing chronic dry eye. But, still...I closed my dry eyes and waited for Mom's response.

"Well, it's a shame that nobody else from the family can go up there," she said.

"Mom, you know I can't—"

"I know, I know." She huffed. "You've been hiding down here for ten years. Why should I expect you to go and visit your poor, sick grandfather now?"

"He's not poor or sick, Mom. Merely maimed. And you know my leaving had nothing to do with him."

"I'm just going to have to hire a home health aide," she went on, ignoring me. "Even though, you know how he gets with strangers. You remember Greta, don't you?"

Greta was the housekeeper Mom had hired for him a few years back. As soon as he'd found out she was coming, Grandpa had hidden every potential valuable in the house beneath his mattress, which Greta found the first time she attempted to change the sheets.

"Of course, I remember Greta. And I *would* go, Mom, if only—"

"No, no," she interrupted. "He'll just have to deal with it. His wrist will be healed in a few weeks, anyway. And if the help *does* steal all his belongings, it'll just make the move that much easier on us."

"The move?" I furrowed my eyebrows. She'd always talked about moving Grandpa down here in an abstract sort of way. But this...this sounded certain.

"I've already looked into it, Amy. There's a nice assisted living facility right here in West Chester. He'd have his own room, three good meals a day, housekeeping..."

"Have *you* forgotten about Greta?"

She ignored me. "We'll have to notify the Parkers before putting the house on the market, but selling it will cover the cost of assisted living for quite a few years."

My stomach churned at the mention of the Parkers, and at the thought of selling our historic, two-family Victorian home. That house had been in our family for generations, and Grandpa had transferred ownership of it to my mother after Gram had died. It was in the most fantastic location, overlooking the town common, and the view from the turret during fall foliage season was like nothing else. Grandpa had grown up in that house, as had my mother and my uncle Pete—who now lived in Utah—and then me. The Parkers were our downstairs neighbors for as long as I could remember—Rebecca, her mother, and her two boys, Kit and Riley.

"I can probably take some time off during the New Year's clearance events," she continued. "Doreen or Jane can fill in for me. It's not like they need to waste their top talent selling the same junk nobody wanted last year!" She snickered into the phone, Grandpa's plight momentarily taking a backseat to her ginormous ego. "Anyway," she cleared her throat, "your father and I will go up there, pack up his things, maybe have a big yard sale..."

I pictured my mother sweeping coldly through the house like some sort of Wayne Szalinski packing machine—mechanical arms scooping Grandpa and a couple of his shirts into a box and mailing him off to an assisted living facility in a state he didn't know. I saw all his belongings spread out across the lawn, heartlessly slapped with neon yard sale price stickers, and it made my heart sink.

Poor Grandpa. He must have been so embarrassed, sitting there in his Jeep, half-in, half-out of Dunkin' Donuts, his wrist snapped like a twig and everybody staring. The poor guy probably didn't even get his chocolate glazed. And now suddenly everything was in jeopardy just because he'd made one tiny mistake. Gas instead of brake.

It could have happened to anybody.

"Wait," I said, another horribly depressing thought occurring to me. "What about Pumpkin Everything?"

When my grandmother passed away many years ago, Grandpa had taken over the operation of her beloved country store on Main Street.

Mom sighed. "We'll have to sell that, too, Amy. Grandpa only took it over because he thought Gram would haunt him if he let it go. But it's too much for him now. He's only been opening for a few hours a day, a few days a week. At this rate, I doubt he'll be able to keep up with the rent much longer. It's got to go."

It's got to go. There wasn't an ounce of nostalgia in her voice. Sure, we'd both left Autumnboro behind, but it had been a harder step for me. I'd loved growing up in that town, and I still dreamed about my view from the turret and the smell of autumn leaves as I walked across the common, kicking them up around my feet. Not Mom, though. Love for Autumnboro had clearly skipped a generation. I'd asked her once if she ever missed it and she'd replied with, *About as much as I miss my debilitating menstrual cramps.* Mom had had big city dreams. Big city dreams that were somehow fulfilled by hosting infomercials in the middle of Pennsylvania. But I couldn't fault her for that. The heart wants what the heart wants. But what about Grandpa's heart? It would crush him to not only have to leave his home but to sell the store that Gram had left in his care.

"But Pumpkin Everything is a landmark," I argued. "It's a fixture on Main Street! The town wouldn't even know what to do with itself if it closed!"

"Oh please. They sell scented candles not cures for cancer. I'm sure the town would manage. *Somehow.*"

"But it belongs in our family!" I cried, feeling panicky. "And so does that house." Through all the panic, the words sounded a bit hollow to my own ears. I hadn't been back to Autumnboro in a decade. Not even once. Mom and Dad drove up to New Hampshire to visit Grandpa a few times a year without me, and I saw him when he flew down to Pennsylvania for the holidays, but that was it. What right did I have to say such things?

Yet, I'd had my reasons for staying away.

After all these years, Kit Parker still lived in the downstairs unit, and I couldn't go back and face him. Not after the way I'd treated him during the most difficult time in his life, when he'd been at his most vulnerable. I saw those eyes and that pleading look of abandonment that had appeared right before I'd skipped town. That familiar twang of guilt rose again in my stomach, but this time it was coupled with a hearty dose of Grandpa-guilt. If I hadn't run off to Penn State, we would never have left him behind either. None of this would be happening right now.

"What do you want from me, huh?" asked Mom, her voice uncharacteristically gentle. "I finally have my dream career down here. Unless you're willing to pack your things and go up there—which you've made perfectly clear you are *not*—then I've run out of choices. The house and the store, they've always been the center of your grandparents' life, Amy. Not mine."

I wasn't sure how to respond. I glanced at my wedding dress, still hanging on the door to the hall closet. I hadn't let myself put it away yet. I'd actually *moved* it into the living room from the bedroom so I'd be forced to look at it more often. Some demented part of me felt that I deserved to stare at it, night after night, regretting the life choices that had led me to Pennsylvania and straight into the arms of my cheating scumbag ex-fiancé. If only I'd stayed with Kit...if only I'd tried a bit harder...yet, with all that regret, I'd never actually considered going back.

Unless you're willing to pack your things and go up there.

Was I? Was I finally willing? Before Grandpa had gunned it

through a Dunkin' Donuts, my plan was to simply go on staring at blank Word documents, regretting my life choices, and waiting for it all to course correct into something tolerable. But now, things were happening very quickly. If I didn't move quickly too, Mom might sell everything out from under me—and with glee. But going back to Autumnboro? Yikes. As much as I loved growing up there, the thought of facing up to my past gave me the cold sweats.

"Well?" asked Mom, after I didn't reply for a good fifteen seconds. I was actually surprised she'd waited that long.

"Does Grandpa still do the scarecrows?"

"What?"

"You know, the scarecrows."

Every fall, after the first round of leaves had been raked into piles, Grandpa, Kit, Riley, and I would spend an entire weekend stuffing scarecrows. Grandpa provided bags of old clothing, hats, and shoes that he picked up from the local thrift shop, and the four of us sat outside in the crisp mountain air, drinking apple cider and hot chocolate, stuffing and sewing and turning it all into a motley cast of characters. We'd put the scarecrows on the front porch and all around the front yard—sitting them in wicker chairs, on railings, in the tire swing. It was quite the display. We even put some on the roof. People walking the town common would stop to take pictures, and every few years our house would end up in the newspaper. One year we even made it into the *Union Leader*.

"Oh, *that*," Mom said as if she were remembering a small-town murder scandal rather than my most treasured childhood memory. "Who would he still be doing that with?"

I shrugged. "I dunno. I always sort of hoped that he'd kept up the tradition with Kit and Riley, even as adults."

"That would be weird."

Right. Better that a scarecrow-less Grandpa sit alone in his empty pizza box-infested house until my mother drags him off to assisted living, severing my last connection to Autumnboro—and Kit Parker—forever than to be *weird*.

I stood and looked at myself in the mirror above the couch, twisting my hair up into a loose bun and letting it drop back down. My wedding dress was visible over my left shoulder, like a creepy, headless ghost bride from a horror film. Knowing what I had to do, I thought over the words I was about to say, and what they would ultimately mean for me. I swallowed down the resulting anxiety.

"I'll do it," I said, not quite loudly enough for her to actually hear.

"Excuse me?"

"I'll do it," I repeated with more confidence. "I'll pack my things, and I'll go up there, and I'll take care of Grandpa. I'll get him back on his feet and I'll check on the store. I'll make sure the house is safe and that he's taking his meds and whatever else you need. And maybe...maybe he won't need to move just yet. We don't need to rush into selling anything yet, right? Just...just let me see what I can do. Please?"

There was a long pause on the other end. Either she was contemplating what I'd said, or she'd passed out cold on the floor.

"How soon can you leave?" she asked at last, sounding a bit far away. She may have actually been flat on her back surrounded by QVC medics.

I told her I could be on the road the next morning, then hung up and sat on the couch for a long time, alternating between silently pondering what on Earth had just happened, and shouting rhetorical, swear-filled questions out into the universe. Still, I knew I had made the right choice. Maybe I would feel differently once I was pulling into Grandpa's driveway and Kit Parker was glaring at me from the front porch, but right now, I knew I couldn't abandon Grandpa in his time of need. I couldn't let my mother whisk him off to assisted living facility, in another state, without at least trying to keep him in his own home. When I was young he'd always put my joy ahead of his own, and now it was my turn to return the favor.

2

I never should have listened to Google Maps.

It meant well, I realize that. By directing me up the scenic route, it was trying to help me avoid a major traffic jam on the interstate. What it also helped me avoid, however, was any chance of rapid assistance should my car suddenly lurch forward like a cat with a hairball, clouds of smoke pouring out from beneath the hood. Google probably didn't even care what it had done to me. Just another dumb human to recalculate into an oblivion. *Moving on! Too-da-loo!*

I'd been sitting alone in the grass on the side of the road for forty-five minutes, only a few miles short of Autumnboro. I'd had enough cell phone reception to call AAA for help, but they were certainly taking their sweet time sending somebody out to get me. They were probably overloaded with calls from Google Maps victims. It was just as well. I'd been hoping to sneak stealthily into town via a deserted side street, so I wasn't exactly dying to get paraded down Main Street in a clunky old tow truck.

I kept glancing back into the woods, expecting a moose or bear to come ambling out. Autumnboro was pretty far up in

New Hampshire—right in the heart of the White Mountains—so it wasn't out of the question. At this time of year, they were probably stocking up on food, and what better food to grab than a defenseless hunk of meat just sitting there in the grass? Although, I couldn't recall anyone ever being eaten by a moose. Bears, sure. But bears didn't collect food for winter, did they? It would probably go bad while they were hibernating. It's not as if they sat around their caves salting meat like the Pilgrims.

I sighed as I watched the other cars zipping past. They were probably filled with sweater-clad leaf-peepers, happily bickering over radio stations and speed limits. Four short months ago, I thought that I, too, would be joining the ranks of the sweater-clad leaf-peepers, happily bickering with my husband—Orion Corcoran. I know, I should have realized way earlier than four months before the wedding that marrying someone with a name like Orion Corcoran couldn't possibly lead to anything good. But he was handsome, and athletic, and welp, here we are.

Even after all the years I'd lived in New Hampshire, I'd never been stranded alone on the side of a road before. I'd barely even had my driver's license before moving away for college. I took a deep breath and tried to force myself to think about something else. Someone else. I sounded like the intro to *Arrow*. *I must become someone else. I must become...something else.* That made me smile a bit, and I spent the next few minutes thinking about Oliver Queen, all suited up in a pair of tight black leather pants before my thoughts eventually drifted back to Kit Parker and my smile pretty much disintegrated. I'd already spent a good part of my seven-hour drive thinking about him and obsessively rehearsing what I would say when we finally met.

I plucked a dandelion out of the grass and rolled it between my fingers. We'd been a complicated thing, Kit and me. We'd had an idyllic boy-next-door, best-friends-to-romance type situation going on for years before everything changed, literally overnight. Kit's mother passed away suddenly from a heart attack the summer before our senior year. After that, he went so quickly from my funny, eternally optimistic boyfriend, to Kit Parker 2.0—a cold shadow of himself, filled with emotions that I couldn't begin to understand. I tried for months to bring him back around, thinking that my love should have been enough to help him fight through his depression. But it wasn't. The fact that I wasn't enough to make him happy was a tough pill to swallow for a seventeen-year-old girl.

As senior year went on, things only got worse. Kit's grades started dropping and he began cutting classes. He refused any sort of help from anybody and didn't want to talk about how he was feeling—even with me. And then, in January, when talk of the senior prom was just starting up, he told me that he wasn't going. He knew I'd been picking out dresses and planning for it for years. He knew I'd been planning to go to it with *him* for years. Yet, as I sat on his bed that dreary afternoon, staring at the back of his head as he tapped sullenly at his computer, he told me that he couldn't bring himself to suffer through it. *Suffer through it*. The words hurt, even now. After everything I'd put up with—his moods, his snarky remarks—he couldn't do this one thing for me. I'd hoped that after such a rough year, the senior prom might be a relief. That it might be one night for us to let loose and bring us closer again.

But he didn't think that he could suffer through it.

That had been the final straw. Such a shallow thing to be a final straw, in comparison to everything he'd been through—I knew that, and I hated myself for it—but I'd had enough, and I ended it. It was then, when I finally ended things between us, that I saw that flicker of emotion come back into his eyes. That desperate, pleading look of abandonment. A look that suggested that maybe, at zero hour, he did still feel something for me. But he said nothing. He let me go. The next day, I accepted my admissions offer from Penn State, a blessed seven hours away from Autumnboro.

My first semester, I met Orion—business major, lacrosse player, and obvious rebound guy—while the guilt I carried for breaking up with Kit continued eating away at me. Perhaps that was why I stayed with someone like Orion for so long. Had almost allowed myself to marry him.

At the sight of a tow truck slowly making its way up the breakdown lane, I dropped the dandelion on the grass and shot to my feet. Finally! I wrapped my arms tightly around my chest as the driver pulled the truck in front of my car, backed up a few feet, and rolled down the window. A pumpkin-headed scarecrow, holding a pair of jumper cables, was painted on the passenger door. *Autumnboro Towing*, it read beneath its splayed-out straw feet. That was our town mascot—a creepy scarecrow with a smiling pumpkin head and possibly murderous intentions. Autumnboro's answer to Mayor McCheese.

"Amy?" called out the driver, his eyes squinted. A note of recognition in his voice. "Amy Evangeline Fox?"

"Yes. That's me," I said, raking my fingers through my wind-blown hair. I didn't remember giving my über long middle name to the AAA lady. "Thank you for coming."

He stepped out of the truck, slammed the door, and walked around to meet me on the grass. I bit back a laugh as I took in his red buffalo check flannel shirt, puffy black vest, and jeans. Northern New Hampshire couldn't have sent a more generic ambassador. He was tall, with a short, scruffy beard, dark blond hair, and—

I sucked in my breath as I met his eyes. Not because they were a heart-stopping shade of molten chocolate, or a paralyzing, Edward Cullen shade of amber, but because they were a simple, soft shade of green that I'd been hoping to avoid at least until I'd managed to cross the town line. I mean, what were the odds? In a town of five thousand, quite good, I supposed. Crikey.

"Kit?" I breathed, squinting up at him against the backdrop of a brilliant blue autumn sky. He'd changed so much. The high school boy with the sweet face and the neatly kept dirty blond hair had been replaced by this more rugged, more lumberjacky model.

Kit Parker 3.0. Holy moly.

TURN THE PAGE FOR A PEEK AT LOVE NOTES IN REINDEER FALLS

1

I had been racing steadily toward rock bottom when the note arrived. It had come in a plain white envelope, the handwriting shaky and unrecognizable. No return address. I'd toyed with the idea that it was from a secret admirer or a kidnapper. Kidnapper was more likely, the way things had been going. Perhaps Mom and Dad had been taken hostage and this ransom note was their only chance at survival. I had no money with which to pay anybody any sort of ransom, so I'd torn it open with bated breath and hoped for the best.

I saw right away that the note wasn't spelled out with letters cut from the pages of a magazine. Rather, it was from Annabeth Pond, my choir director from back home. Miss Annabeth had taught choir at both the junior high and high school, and had been in charge of the town's annual Christmas show. She was more like family to me, than a teacher, and it was with much guilt that I realized I hadn't spoken with her in a few years. As I read through the note, the words *kidney donor* and *something of great importance to ask* jumped out at me as if they were written in flashing neon, rather than ordinary blue pen.

I'd immediately booked a flight, thrown some clothes into a

suitcase, and told the post office to hold my mail. It was with a passing moment of gloom that I realized I had nobody else to notify. No boyfriend. No close friends who would wonder where I'd gone off to. No job. Like I said, rock bottom coming up fast.

Free as a bird, I flew from Boston, Massachusetts to my tiny hometown of Reindeer Falls, Tennessee. Technically, I flew to Knoxville and drove the rest of the way. Reindeer Falls doesn't exactly have its own airport, unless you want to count the patch of grass in the town square designated as Santa's Landing Strip. Reindeer Falls is certainly unique. One Christmas Eve, way back in the eighteen-hundreds—when the town was simply known as Milford—the mayor had indulged in a bit too much eggnog and claimed to have witnessed a majestic reindeer stepping out from behind the town waterfall. It was all he could talk about for weeks, eventually going so far as re-naming the town so that nobody would ever forget the fact that he'd probably just seen a really big deer. Regardless, the town embraced the idea, and soon just about everything had a Christmas theme.

I was sitting now in Miss Annabeth's cozy living room, waiting while she made a pot of tea. Burl Ives—her plump black cat with the big white paws—was rubbing against my ankles. Burl had been only a kitten the last time I'd seen him, and I enjoyed getting reacquainted while I waited.

Miss Annabeth had sent letters to all three of us—me, Emma, and Michelle—the girls she'd bonded for life with that silly friendship bracelet ritual back in sixth grade. We'd just finished our first ever performance of "I'll Be Home for Christmas" at the community center's Christmas show, and Miss Annabeth had led us all outside into the snow. She said that she'd watched the three of us growing closer over the past few months, and that she wanted to share something with us that she'd once done with her own group of childhood friends.

She pulled three of the woven friendship bracelets that we'd made earlier in the day out of her pocket, and tied one onto each of our wrists. Then, while she read us the old poem that she and her friends had written about friendship being a precious thing, made and woven out of string...we stood there, giggling nervously, but feeling like something truly magical was in the air.

As it turned out, those two girls became my closest friends all throughout junior high and high school. As silly as that bracelet ritual seemed, I've always felt fortunate to have been a part of it—even if we did drift apart after high school. Emma got into modeling and ended up in New York City. Michelle went off to college in California, where she ended up staying. While the three of us still kept in touch by email, it had been a few years since I'd seen either of them in person.

I looked around Miss Annabeth's once immaculate home—now filling up with unwashed dishes, a thick layer of dust on the coffee table, a basket of laundry by the basement door—and I wondered how she was still managing to get by on her own. I suddenly felt guilty that she was in the kitchen making tea for me, a perfectly healthy twenty-six-year-old woman. I stood up and headed toward the kitchen to help, when she appeared in the doorway carrying a tray covered in teacups and cookies.

"Let me take that," I said, gently taking the tray from her hands and setting it on the coffee table. "Sit down." I gingerly put a hand on her shoulder and directed her to the couch. She sat down with a sigh.

"Oh, that's better," she said. "Thank you, dear."

I sat in the wingback chair opposite and looked her over. Shoulder-length silver hair. Minimal wrinkles. She looked tired, and a bit dark beneath her blue eyes, but still elegant. In another life, I always imagined her sweeping about in a Hollywood mansion, sipping martinis and telling stories of her useless ex-husbands, one eye firmly on the pool boy.

"The tea is quite hot," she said. "While we let it cool, would you mind?" She motioned across the living room to the upright piano against the wall.

"Oh," I said, taken aback. "I don't know. It's been so long."

"I'm not asking you to perform at the Grand Ole Opry, dear. Just to play for an old lady in her living room."

I smiled. "Sure, Miss Annabeth."

I walked over and sat nervously down at the piano. I couldn't even remember the last time I had played. I didn't want to make her get up and search for sheet music, so I played the only song that I knew by heart. The theme song from the *Super Mario Bros.* The sound of Miss Annabeth laughing echoed throughout the house as I played, while images of Mario leaping over pipes, fireballs spewing from his hands, flashed through my mind. There were few greater reminders of my childhood. I played the final sad notes as Mario miscalculated a jump and fell to his death, and then I turned around. Miss Annabeth was wiping tears from her eyes.

"Oh, my," she laughed. "I was expecting something dull like 'Moonlight Sonata.' But *that*. That brings back some memories. You girls used to play that game for hours at the community center."

"I know," I said. "That was the whole reason I hung out there. Mom and Dad wouldn't buy me video games. I did, however, have a hoop and a stick." I walked over and sat down next to her on the couch. She brushed a stray piece of my long, auburn hair over my shoulder, her hand cold as it brushed against my cheek.

"Beautiful girl," she said. "You've always been able to make me laugh."

I smiled, happy to have brought a few minutes of joy to Miss Annabeth, although I sensed that the conversation was about to take a serious turn.

"But now we do need to get down to business," she continued. "The reason I asked all of you girls to come home is because I have a small favor to ask."

"Of course. You need a kidney."

Miss Annabeth looked at me as if I'd totally lost my mind. "Good lord, no!"

"What do you mean *no*? You need one, don't you?"

"Well, *yes*. But I would never ask for one from you girls." She took a sip of tea, a bit angrily. "I'm on the donor list, Caitlin, and that's that. That part of it is none of your concern."

I sank back into the couch, somewhat let down. Somewhat relieved. Somewhat ticked off that I'd blown my rent money on a plane ticket...for what?

"What is it that you need, then?" I asked slowly, through gritted teeth.

"My request is much simpler than that," she sighed. "All I want is for you girls to perform again at the Christmas show. You've drifted much too far apart lately. The friendship bonds you formed that special night have become much too loose over the years. You do remember the bracelets, don't you?" She looked at me accusingly, one eyebrow raised. I glanced down at my bare wrist and nodded guiltily.

"Well," she continued, "it would give me great peace to know that you girls are going to be there for each other after...after I'm gone." Her voice broke slightly. "In fact, it would make the entire town happy to see you girls together again."

The Christmas show had always been quite the event in our tiny town. After that first performance of "I'll Be Home for Christmas"—with me on piano and the other girls singing—the three of us decided to turn it into an annual tradition. The town loved it. After our final performance, right before we'd graduated from high school and gone our separate ways, the *Reindeer*

Falls Gazette had even printed an article lamenting the end of an era.

We were sort of a big deal.

But as much as I wanted to give Miss Annabeth peace of mind, I would rather walk through Harvard Square in my graduation cap and underwear than play the piano in front of such a large audience again. Sure, I could play a decent rendition of the *Super Mario Bros.* theme, but I hadn't actually sat down and practiced in forever. Over the past eight years, music had taken a back seat to everything else in my life.

"Have the other girls agreed to do it?" I asked.

"You're the first one who's been kind enough to come see me, Caity," she said, taking a small sip of tea, her eyes shifting toward the floor. "But when they do come, if I could tell them that *you'd* already agreed to it, well..."

I loved Miss Annabeth, but she could be a manipulative little bugger when she wanted. She once reverse-psychologied me into agreeing to accompany the Reindeer Falls Men's Club's performance of *Show Boat*. That was in tenth grade, and I still haven't quite forgiven her. But, for the most part, she was a sweetheart.

"You know I never could say no to you," I sighed. "So, yes. For you, Miss Annabeth, I'll do it."

"Wonderful!" she said, reaching over and squeezing my hand. "I'm so glad."

As soon as I saw that familiar sparkle return to her eyes, I knew I'd made the right decision.

"There *is* one more thing," she added. "I didn't want to mention it in the letter, on top of everything else, but the town just doesn't have the money to keep the community center open much longer. After this year's Christmas show, they're planning to close it down."

"Oh, no," I said, frowning. "Isn't there anything we can do?"

"We've done some fundraising," she said, nodding thoughtfully. "That's how we've managed to stay open as long as we have. But there are only so many boxes of cookies and rolls of wrapping paper we can sell. Especially with money being so tight for everybody around here."

My shoulders slumped. Everything truly seemed to be falling apart all at once. First my boyfriend, then my job. Now the community center, where I'd forged my closest childhood friendships, was going to be nothing but a rundown empty shell the next time I came back to Reindeer Falls. Worst of all was the thought of Miss Annabeth no longer being with us. Tears stung my eyes as the sad reality sank in.

"We'll figure something out," I said. "I promise. And you'll get that kidney donor. Just relax and try to stay positive. If there's one place destined for a Christmas miracle, it's a town called Reindeer Falls."

"That is true," she said, patting my hand and taking a sip of tea. "Thank goodness we're not still called Milford."

2

My bed was in there somewhere. It had to be. Mom had told me over the phone, just last week, that all my things were still where I'd left them. She'd also said that I was welcome to come home at any time—didn't I *know* that I never needed to ask? —and that there would be a Christmas tree, a home-cooked meal, and a warm bed waiting for me. Only, standing in the doorway of my childhood bedroom, gazing into the overflowing abyss of Amazon shipping boxes, knickknacks, clothing, stuffed animals, books, and who knew what else, there wasn't a warm bed in sight. The home-cooked meal was also starting to seem unlikely.

Unless...

There was a large, vaguely rectangular mound in the corner of the room. My eyes followed the gentle sloping of clutter that rose up from the floor and ended just below the window. I stepped carefully into the room, parkouring my way across the various items, trying my best to avoid stepping too heavily in any one spot. Something hard crunched beneath my heel. I hoped there weren't any pets hiding in here. Our family cat, Pickles, had passed away years ago and as far as I knew, Mom and Dad had never gotten a replacement. The last thing I needed was to hear a crunch and a meow as I put down my foot.

With a leap, and a mercifully meowless landing, I made it to the corner of the room. I tossed a huge pile of clothing off the rectangular mound, revealing the pink and orange patchwork of my teenaged bedspread. I could only see a few square inches of it, but it was definitely there. Mom hadn't been lying. Which meant that the rest of my stuff was also still there. Just...buried.

I sank down onto the bed, a life raft amongst the hoard, and surveyed my room from this new angle. Mom and Dad may have turned the floor space of my bedroom into a chaotic catchall, but anything I had hung from the walls had managed to stay intact. A homemade photo collage still hung over the bureau, the faces of my two best friends smiling back at me. Bracelet Buddies forever. We were surrounded by colorful words cut from magazines: *Remember the Times! Besties!* I wondered how many of my old friends had returned home to find similar reminders of their youth. Probably just me. Normal parents would have packed up all this junk years ago. Normal parents would have thrown it all away once their child had moved out.

It had been two years since I'd been home—and yes, I cringed after I'd worked out the calculations. Visiting me on the East Coast was always the more exciting option for Mom, Dad, and my little brother Nate, so it had always been easy for me to avoid coming home to Tennessee. As for the holidays, I spent last Christmas and this past Thanksgiving with my ex-boyfriend Ben's wealthy family up in cozy, picturesque Vermont. He took me on a sleigh ride with horses, and jingle bells, and right on cue, a dusting of snow had swirled down from the sky. It was legit holiday magic and I'd arrived back in Boston with the sense that all was right with the world.

Two days later, a love note written by one of Ben's female

coworkers fell into my lap. I'd been happily watching a rerun of *Twin Peaks,* lost in the Douglas firs and cherry pie, when Ben came in, stood next to the couch, and the note literally fell out of his pocket and into my lap. Legit holiday magic over. Three days later I lost my job. The thought of returning home for Christmas, single and unemployed, made it a bit hard to breathe. That was, until Miss Annabeth's note arrived and the decision was made for me.

Growing up in the Cook household, things had always been somewhat cramped and hard to breathe. Various pieces of furniture that Mom and Dad planned to restore and sell in their antique shop, Christmas Past, were always found around the house. Rocking chair in the bathroom. Floor to ceiling mirror wedged beside the refrigerator. There was a period of time when we ate all of our meals around a pair of wooden skis. For most of my childhood, it was quirky and fun. It had been manageable. Junk came in, and junk went out. It was my parents' livelihood and it had worked. But as the years went on, there came a noticeable turning of the tides where the junk came in, but it didn't always go out. What had once been quirky and fun had started giving me anxiety and claustrophobia.

You used to not be able to tell from the outside of the house what was happening on the inside. Driving down our rural road, our big white farmhouse with the black shutters looked just like any other. Sure, it was a little shabby and a little rustic—but it mostly looked homey and lived in. But as soon as I pulled into the driveway after two years away, I noticed the difference immediately. Things that didn't belong outside had begun creeping onto the porch. An old recliner. A rowing machine. An outdated, boxy computer monitor covered in spider webs and leaves. On closer inspection, I saw that it was *my* computer monitor. The one I had typed all my high school papers on. My first reaction was to feel sorry for it. What was once a state-of-the-art piece of computing equipment, integral to my education, had been abandoned to the outdoors to become a housing development for mice. My second reaction, felt deep in the pit of my stomach, was dread. Because the only reason a computer monitor would be out on the front porch, was if there just wasn't enough room for it anywhere else.

The sound of a key in the lock downstairs pulled me quickly back to the present.

"Caity?" shouted Mom. "Are you here?"

"Coming!" I jumped off the bed and made my way down the stairs. My heart was suddenly bursting with excitement at the thought of seeing my family.

"Sweetheart!" said Mom. She stepped deftly around various piles of things, using a path that only she could see, and swept me into a hug.

"Hi, Mom," I said into her neck. Same old Mom. Dressed in a thick wool cardigan and smelling like a flea market.

"Hi, Dad," I said, tripping over a pile of extension cords as I went to him for a hug. Same old Dad. Dressed like a flea market and smelling like a thick wool cardigan. I'd missed them both.

"Nathan," I said, stepping back and gently punching my brother on the shoulder. To my surprise, he stepped forward to give me a hug. Nate was sixteen, and I felt a wave of concern due to the fact that he has *never* wanted to hug me.

"It's good to see you," he mumbled.

Or said that it was good to see me.

"It's good to see you, too." I took a step back and looked up into his face. He was taller than me now, and a bit gangly. He was quickly becoming a miniature version of Dad, minus the mustache. "How are you?"

"I spent the morning at an estate sale with Mom and Dad. How do you think I am?" On that note, he loped off toward the stairs, using the same path over the junk as had Mom. I still couldn't see it.

"Estate sale?" I looked from Mom to Dad and back again. "How'd that go?" I didn't see anybody carrying any plastic Thank You bags, which was a good sign. There seemed to be more than enough stuff already in the house—never mind what they probably had at the store—to keep them in business for the next twenty years.

"It's all out in the truck," said Dad, grinning.

"All?" My eyes widened. "*Truck*?" Mom and Dad didn't own a truck, as far as I knew.

Mom put her arm lovingly around Dad's shoulders and gave him a shake. "This one just had to have Giles Wilson's International Harvester. He's had his eye on it for years. Giles finally sold it to him for three grand. Said he needed the money to pay medical bills and your father, the old ghoul, he jumped at the chance."

"I tried to offer him five!" protested Dad, throwing his hands out in front of him. "But he wouldn't hear of it!"

"Go have a look," said Mom, motioning to the front door.

I stared at them both for a moment—they looked as if they had just brought their third child into the world—before making my way to the door. Mater from *Cars* was parked in the driveway, minus the buckteeth. The truck was painted a rusty shade of red, with retro aqua hubcaps, and the words "Wilson's Feed Store" still stenciled on the side in white lettering. The back was piled high with a heap of old furniture, and I stifled a giggle at the thought of the three of them stuffed into the front seat, bouncing on home like the Beverly Hillbillies. Poor Nate.

"Dining set, armoire, boxes full of jewelry. Esther Adams passed away last month. Ninety-seven years old. Her daughter's selling everything," said Dad, in his clipped way of speaking. He joined me by the door. "No choice sometimes. Folks are having a rough time around here. Especially this time of year."

I looked up at Dad in concern. Miss Annabeth had also mentioned money being tight lately, but my parents had never mentioned money troubles to me before. Our family had always lived simply, and with the tourism spillover from Gatlinburg, they'd always had a fairly steady stream of business.

"Your mom and I are hanging in there," he added, giving me a reassuring squeeze around the shoulders. "We're hanging in there. You might even say we've been reaping the benefits!" He nodded toward Giles Wilson's truck filled with Esther Adams' worldly possessions.

"He's a ghoul!" shouted Mom from the living room.

Dad chuckled as he headed outside to unload the truck.

"So, Mom," I said, joining her in the living room. "Things have changed a bit since I've last been here." I gestured from the couch, where there wasn't a single place to sit, to the stack of boxes obscuring the picture window.

"Oh," said Mom, looking vaguely around, her eyes skimming over objects her brain had filtered out. "I suppose the place could use some tidying up. We're just so busy doing restorations and school things with Nate..."

"And a tree! Mom, there's no Christmas tree!"

"It's still early. We'll get one."

"You promised me a tree." I made a mopey little girl face.

"We'll *get* one, Caity. We just need to...clear a space." She looked optimistically toward the corner where we'd always displayed our tree. It was presently occupied by a fortress of boxes marked *Doll Heads*.

"Come on," said Mom, steering me out of the living room and changing the subject. "I'll make you some coffee and we can catch up before the concert!"

The annual holiday band concert was being held tonight at

the high school. Nate played the trumpet. I knew it was just a lame high school concert, but I was still pretty excited to go. I had performed in it every year that I was in high school. I was a flute player, as well as the piano accompanist for the choir and jazz band. I was sure they'd be playing all the same arrangements of all the same holiday songs that I remembered. Everybody would be dressed in the same uniform of black pants, white shirts, and red bow ties. There would be holiday decorations and a table of baked goods for sale by the music boosters.

There would also be Shane.

"You know who the band director is now, don't you?" asked Mom, reading my mind as she moved things around, attempting to locate the coffeemaker. I watched as she pulled a box of K-Cups out of the microwave.

"Um, yep."

"Shane Mitchell!" she exclaimed. My response was clearly not dismissive enough. She suddenly stopped what she was doing and turned to look at me, her face bearing the same expression of scrunched-up concern as when I told her I had chosen Harvard over Vanderbilt. "You know, I didn't even think that it might be awkward for you, seeing him again."

"It's no big deal, Mom. He'll be with the band. He probably won't even notice me. Besides, we've kept in touch on Facebook."

By "we've kept in touch on Facebook," I meant that I'd stared at all his public photos without having the nerve to send him a friend request. I certainly didn't want to run into him at the concert, but there was no easy way to avoid going. Nate had a trumpet solo and it would hurt his feelings if I skipped. Besides, I was more nostalgic for my band days than I was nervous about bumping into Shane. The odds were slim.

"I never did get into that Facebook stuff," muttered Mom, fishing around in a metal tin, pulling out receipts, coupons, and finally a handful of sugar packets.

Probably because the computer's out on the front porch, I thought, taking a few sugar packets and finding myself a spot at the kitchen island. I rested my coffee mug in the space between a pair of antique snowshoes.

"You working on fixing these up?" I asked.

Mom looked down at the snowshoes with a furrowed brow. She had clearly stopped noticing they were there ages ago.

"Eventually," she said, with a dismissive wave. "So, tell me, Caity, what's this all about? Coming home like this out of the blue? Not that I'm not grateful. I'm thrilled to have you home. We all are. This past Christmas and Thanksgiving just weren't the same."

"I know, Mom," I said, my chest filling with regret. "I'm sorry about that. And this year, well"—I paused to take a sip of coffee — "to be honest, I didn't think I'd have the money for a plane ticket."

"They're paying you at that job of yours, aren't they? Please don't tell me it's another unpaid internship."

"I had *one* unpaid internship, Mom. And that was four years ago. Of course, they pay me now. How do you think I've been surviving on my own all these years?"

Mom just shrugged. "Well then, what happened?"

I sighed. "Three days after Ben and I broke up, I lost my job."

"Oh, no," she said. "I'm so sorry."

"It's not like publishing history books was my dream job," I said, shrugging. "I'll find something else. Anyway, even if I had the money to fly home, I was embarrassed to show up here single and unemployed. I was considering making something up about going to Vermont again. I almost told you that Ben and I had gotten back together."

"That boy *does not* deserve a second chance." Mom's concerned face was back with a vengeance, moments away from calling my father into the house for an intervention.

"It was a lie, Mom. Remember?"

"Right. Good." She put down the napkin she'd been twisting between her fingers and her face lit up. "Does this mean you're moving back home?"

I ignored the question. "That's when I got the note in the mail from Miss Annabeth. She told me that she needs a kidney transplant." I fought back tears as I said the words out loud. "She's asked Michelle, Emma, and me to perform again at the Christmas show. She wants to see it again, just in case this is her last chance."

"Oh, Caity," said Mom, putting one hand over her mouth. "I had no idea."

"She doesn't want anybody to feel sorry for her," I sighed. "But she really is sick. And not only that, the community center is running out of money. She told me that after the Christmas show, the town is closing it down."

Mom patted my hand and shook her head in sympathy.

"Anyway," I continued. "As soon as I got her note, I packed my bags, used the last of my rent money to buy a plane ticket, and here I am!" I threw my hands in the air.

Mom took a sip of coffee, but I could tell by her eyes that she was smiling behind her mug.

"You have some nerve calling *Dad* an old ghoul," I said. "Tell me, Mom, what part of my favorite teacher being ill, me losing my job, my boyfriend, and my childhood memories, are you smiling about?"

"Don't be morbid, love. I'm not happy about any of that."

"Then what is it?"

"I'll let you in on a little secret," she said. "Even if you were here because the entire East Coast had fallen into the ocean"—she reached across the counter and squeezed me by the wrists—"I'd still be happy to see my daughter."

"Thanks, Mom." I smiled back. Then a thought occurred to

me. "Do you think that if the entire East Coast *were* to fall into the ocean, my student loans would be forgiven?"

Mom shrugged and took another sip of coffee. "Never give up hope, love." She motioned toward the front of the house. "That's how your father got his truck."